Praise for Colette Gale:

"Erotically wicked! Spellbinding! A unique retelling of *The Phantom of the Opera*." — Bertrice Small on *Unmasqued*

"Colette Gale leads us through a labyrinth of dark, extravagant eroticism, to the romance at the story's heart. Grandly conceived, wildly inventive in the smallest details—I for one will never hear harp music in quite the same way again." — Molly Weatherfield, author of *Carrie's Story*.

"Lush and sensual." — Erotica Romance Writers

"Inventive and steamy and clever all at once." — M. J. Rose, author of *The Resurrectionist*

Books by Colette Gale:

The Erotic Adventures of Jane in the Jungle
(published as separate ebook volumes)

Entwined: Jane in the Jungle
Entangled: An Unexpected Menage
Enthralled: The Sex Goddess
Enticed: An Erotic Sacrifice
Enamored: The Submissive Mistress
Enslaved (coming soon)

Unmasqued: An Erotic Novel of The Phantom of the Opera

Master: An Erotic Novel of The Count of Monte Cristo

Bound by Honor: An Erotic Novel of Maid Marian

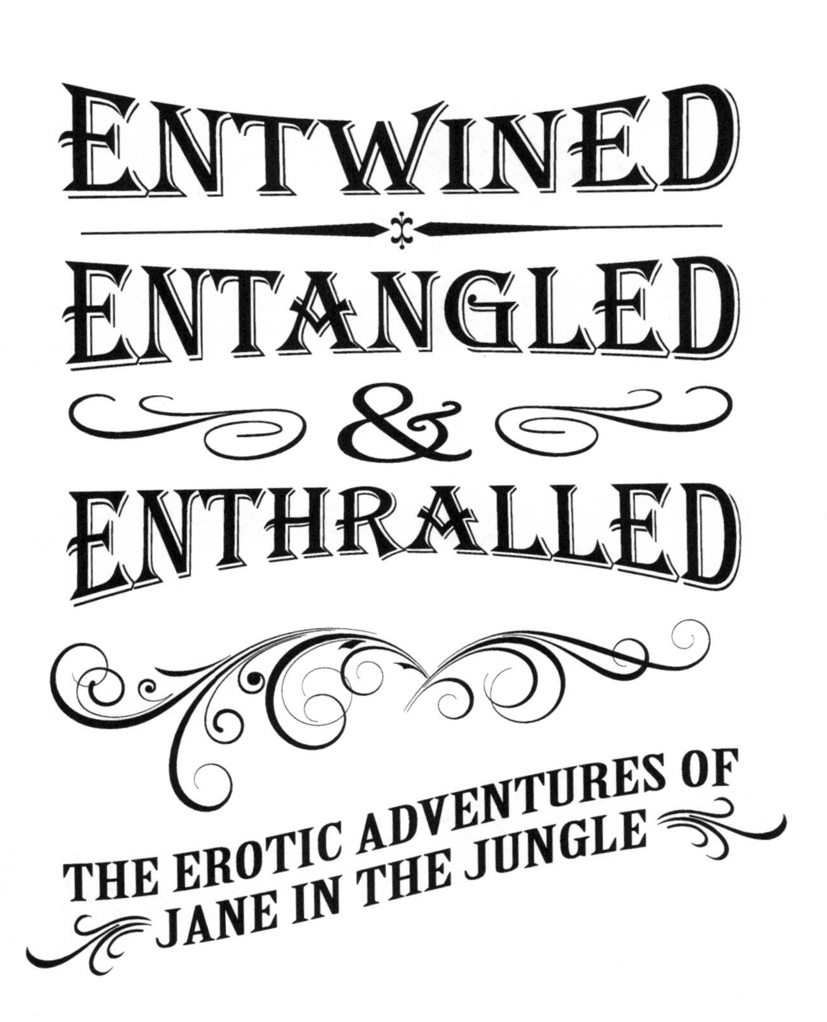

Entwined Entangled & Enthralled

The Erotic Adventures of Jane in the Jungle

Colette Gale

AVID PRESS

ENTWINED, ENTANGLED, and ENTHRALLED were previously published in ebook format only as separate volumes. This is the first time any part of this collection has appeared in print.

Published by Avid Press.
ISBN: 978-1-931419-32-1

Cover design: Kim Killion
Interior design: Dan Keilen

Colette Gale

Dear Reader:

During the late 19th century, the British indulged in much exploration of Africa, searching not only for gold and gemstones, but also for knowledge of this fascinating Dark Continent.

Professor Everett Clemons, the famous lepidopterist, and his daughter Jane were two of the most famous British citizens to embark on these travels, and although Jane published a book of her drawings and notations about the butterflies her father studied during these trips, there remained little information about her own thoughts and adventures—until now.

Recently, I was fortunate enough to come across an old trunk filled with Professor Clemons's journals and butterfly specimens, and there, within, I also found the treasure of Miss Jane Clemons's personal journals.

Because there were so many volumes of her journals, I have chosen to publish a series of short segments over time in order to make them publicly available as quickly and efficiently as possible.

I do hope you'll indulge my decision to follow the popular form of literature from this era and publish Jane's journals as a serialized collection. And, I must warn you: also in the tradition of the times, each episode ends on a cliffhanger.

I hope you find Jane's adventures enlightening, exciting, and titillating as we follow her adventures as a young woman in the Madagascar jungle.

Colette Gale
January 2012

The Coast of Madagascar
1890

MISS JANE CLEMONS WALKED quickly and nimbly down the ship's gangplank that led to a sandy shore. Her skirts billowed and buffeted in the wind and strands of strawberry-blond hair whipped about her face as she looked at the land that would be her home for the next month.

A generous swath of pearly-white sand ranged before her, stretching from one side to the other as far as she could see. The blue ocean, laced with foam, surged onto the beach in a roar of wave after wave. Beyond the flat expanse of sand loomed a lush green jungle. Even from here, she could see brightly colored flowers, thick hanging vines and sturdy lianas, ferns and palms and numerous other unidentifiable flora and fauna. Everything gave the impression of being cool and thick and both dangerous and welcoming.

"It's beautiful!" she said, turning to look over her shoulder at her father, Professor Everett Clemons, as he clumped along behind her.

"Mr. Darkdale has told me that he is certain I shall find a great assortment of butterfly specimens here," puffed Professor Clemons. "I can hardly contain my excitement at seeing all the little beasties in their natural habitat!"

In addition to being short and rotund, he was also carrying a large satchel which Jane knew contained some of his journals and other equipment. The rest of their belongings—trunks of books, scientific implements, household goods, and clothing—would be despatched by the crew-members of *The Fledgling* before that ship set sail.

Other than their two companions, Jane and her father wouldn't see another human—at least, another English speaking one; there could be natives living in the vicinity—for almost a month.

"Lordy, that'ere place looks right gloomy and dark," rumbled Efremina, Jane's maid, as she lumbered down the gangplank. It shook violently, for she was a large, round woman with a loud voice and kind heart. "There be wild animals creepin' through there, and they'll be attackin' us in our beds!"

"Now Miss Efremina, and Miss Clemons," said Kellan Darkdale in his cultured voice, "there's not a thing to worry about as long as I'm here." His stride was long and sure, and he brandished a large shotgun that he'd boasted would fell an elephant with one bullet. "Our quarters will be nearby and high off the ground, for there is an old treehouse made by some survivors of a shipwreck. It'll want for some cleaning," he said, stepping onto the sand and looking meaningfully at Efremina, "but I don't believe it's in too much disrepair."

"Is that where you stayed when Jonathan was here with you?" asked Jane, shielding her eyes against the sun as she looked up at him. "Was it in good repair then?"

"I'm afraid not, Miss Clemons. At that time, we stayed on the ship and came ashore everyday, but we did notice the treehouse. I am certain it still stands, for it was very well-built by those who lived there. They used strong bamboo as well as lumber, along with strips of liana bark and vines to lash the walls together." His gaze lingered on Jane as it often did, traveling down over her buttoned-up bodice and lower. This time, however, his attention strayed longer and heavier and he stood much closer to her than usual.

His regard made her feel a combination of heat and discomfort, for she never knew quite what to make of the way he looked at her. It wasn't the same way Jonathan had gazed upon her—with tenderness and affection.

Oh, poor, *dear* Jonathan.

Jane turned away and wiped her eyes, pretending she'd gotten seaspray in them. It had been three years since Jonathan, her fiance and lover, had disappeared while on an expedition in this very jungle with Kellan Darkdale.

Though she was only twenty at the time, Jane had lost interest in meeting other young men in London after the loss of her love. It had taken her two years to convince her father that he should undertake a butterfly-hunting expedition to the very same place Jonathan had disappeared, and several more months that she should accompany her father. She was determined to find something that would answer her question of what had happened to Jonathan once and for all.

Professor Clemons was never one to deny his only daughter anything that she begged from him, and thus he was completely helpless in the face of her blue-eyed pleadings—especially when she offered to illustrate his studies. Against his better judgment, he'd agreed to allow her to come with him to Africa where he intended to capture and categorize a variety of butterflies.

"My God! Is that a black-tailed pipsqueak?" Professor Clemons exclaimed, pushing past them and dashing off on his short legs.

With an affectionate smile at her parent, Jane stepped past Mr. Darkdale. She enjoyed the way her feet sank into the soft beach and wondered what it would be like to remove her buttoned-up shoes and silk stockings and dig her feet into the warm grains of sand. Her corset, though she wore one, had not been laced tightly since they left London, despite Efremina's grumblings. And, Jane had secretly thought, perhaps once the ship and its crew left and there were only the four of them, she might be able to even unbutton the top of her shirtwaist.

After all, who was here to see her in this vast, remote jungle?

High above, his darkly tanned muscular arm curled easily around the smooth trunk of a tree, a man looked down at the people as they disembarked from the large *thing* that sat floating in the ocean.

It had been a long time since he'd seen others like himself come from the ocean. There were many who lived deep in the jungle, with skin the color of soil and bumpy, coarse hair. But these people came from a different place. They were like the people in the picture books left by some long-ago inhabitant who'd made the odd nest in the trees.

He watched the short, round man with pale skin and sparse white hair as he tripped and nearly fell due to the weight of the bag he carried over one shoulder and the fact that he was too busy looking up and around than to pay attention to where his feet were going. And there was another man, taller and younger, with light skin—skin nearly as light as his own. He carried a long, metal object that gleamed evilly in the sunlight.

There were two other creatures. Women. He remembered the word, for he'd studied the picture books. The two women were as different from each other as the two men were: one was nearly as large and muscular as a young ape, also with pale skin and dark hair. But the other one…she was slender and lithe… and her hair was like golden fire.

The watcher in the trees was immediately fascinated by the second woman, his attention drawn to that fiery beacon of hair. He wondered if it would be warm to the touch, if it would burn his fingers.

He found a thick vine and swung easily and silently, high

in the treetops, following the group of people as they made their way along the beach. They spoke to each other in some language that sounded vaguely familiar to him; so much so that it made his head hurt when he tried to listen. And so he stopped listening and simply followed them as they made their way to the strange nest in the trees…the place where he'd found so many fascinating things.

He perched high above, just off to the side and looked down as they made their way into the nest. He was glad he'd removed all of the interesting items over the years, tucking them away in his own nest that had been fashioned similarly to this one. They were his treasures, and he didn't want anyone seeing them.

Even the woman with the burning hair.

His hand opened and closed, as if he were to touch her right now. He imagined what it would feel like—that smooth, warm, burning covering on her head.

He'd have to wait until night.

JANE FOUND THE TREEHOUSE surprisingly comfortable. It was constructed of bamboo, palm fronds, timber and vines, and was settled in the branches of a massive tree. Due to space constraints among said branches, the dwelling consisted of several levels, with chambers built atop each other like a messy stack of square or rectangle blocks. Ladders or ramps connected each level, with the main floor being kitchen and parlor combined into one large space. Pieces of the walls moved like massive sliding doors to open or close against the weather, and smaller doors allotted privacy to the bedchambers.

By the time the sun was setting, Jane and Efremina had cleaned up all of the rooms, made dinner, and settled their belongings in their respective bedchambers. Papa had gone off with Mr. Darkdale to hunt down a blue-faced tweak he was certain he'd spied in the distance, and they'd returned just as darkness began to fall and the night sounds of the wild animals began in earnest. The roar of some creature that sounded angry and hungry reverberated through the night, sending Efremina scuttling under her bedcovers.

If Jane felt odd about the ship leaving them to continue on its journey, she brushed away any nervousness. Mr. Darkdale, for all his long glances and heavy looks, was well able to protect them, and he'd assured them that the treehouse, with its ladders pulled up, was a very safe place to sleep. However, Efremina had loudly declared she was not about to sleep high up in the trees with the bats, and she'd chosen to make her bed in one of the lower storage rooms, which had no windows.

This left Jane the unexpected pleasure of having a room to herself, and she chose one at the uppermost level. There were two large windows on which tattered curtains had hung, and she'd pulled them down in order to allow the gentle breeze from the ocean to cool the chamber. There was no one but perhaps a black-tailed pipsqueak or one of the bright red and blue birds she'd seen flitting about to see her as she loosened her hair and allowed it to fall in a heavy, waist-length swath.

It felt like heaven to run her fingers through it, massaging her scalp and shaking out the long curls that had been confined by pins all day. Then, lit by the golden glow from a small lantern, Jane began to unbutton her shirtwaist. As each button popped free, she felt the welcome breeze of fresh air cooling her skin until at last she was able to strip it off and hang it on a handy hook fixed on the wall.

Next, she unrolled her stockings, lifting her foot onto the bed in order to keep her skirts out of the way, and wondering why she hadn't done this first of all. Her toes wriggled on the clean, bare floor (she'd need to find something for a rug), freed of their tight, warm confines. Then she removed her skirt and crinoline, and with herself free of those heavy weights, Jane was left only in her corset and chemise. A sense of freedom such that she'd never known back in the confines of Victorian London suffused her, and all at once Jane felt incredibly unencumbered and alive.

She went to stand at the window, her long hair falling out of the opening like Rapunzel's legendary tresses. She could never have done such a bold thing back in London: standing in full view of the window in her unmentionables and letting her hair blow free. The breeze toyed with her curls like that of a lover's fingers, and she drew in a deep breath of the sweet scents of flowers and the tang of ocean.

Jonathan, she thought, looking out into the darkness. *Whatever has befallen you, I pray I'll find the answers so that I may go on with my life knowing you are at peace.*

A knock thumped her door and Jane turned in surprise. She picked up a shawl and draped it over her shoulders before poking her head through the entrance.

"Mr. Darkdale," she said in surprise. What was he doing on the threshold of her room?

"Miss Clemons," he said, his eyes raking over her dishabille. "I came to ensure that you're comfortable for the night, and that your bedchamber is secure."

"I'm perfectly comfortable," she said, her pulse jumping. He was looking at her in such a way that made her feel prickly and unsettled. His face was in shadow, the flickering light from her lantern the only illumination.

The next thing she knew, his foot was between the door and its frame and he was gently but firmly pressuring the door open. "Miss Clemons, I wouldn't feel comfortable taking my own bed until I knew you were settled and safe in here. I'd like to check for snakes—they like to lurk under the bed, you know. And the large spiders and scorpions as well."

"Snakes?" Jane said, her heart thumping. "And spiders?" Much as she didn't wish the man to enter her chamber, she much less preferred the possibility of sharing the room with such creatures. "Perhaps you'd best check, Mr. Darkdale... although Efremina and I did a very thorough job of cleaning. We didn't encounter one snake."

"They come out at night," he said, giving her a long, heavy look.

Jane swallowed hard. She moved back from the door and it opened. Mr. Darkdale stepped in and she edged to the side, watching as he looked beneath the bed. The existing frame had been completed by a goosefeather mattress she'd brought from London, along with several light blankets and a pillow. As she stood near the doorway, Jane could hear the unmistakable sound of her father's snoring cutting through the night.

The realization that her father was dead asleep and her maid too far away to hear anything somehow made her even more nervous to have Mr. Darkdale in her chamber.

As if sensing this, he rose, turning from his perusal under her bed. His dark eyes settled on her and Jane felt her breathing quicken.

"Miss Clemons," he said, advancing toward her.

All at once, she remembered she was garbed only in her chemise and corset, and that her hastily-donned shawl was slipping down from her shoulder. "No spiders or snakes?" she said brightly. "Thank you very much for checking, Mr. Darkdale."

"Kellan. You *must* call me Kellan, Miss Clemons. *Jane*." His voice had dropped into something deep and husky and his eyes did not waver from her person. "We are far from the proprieties of London, and there's no need to maintain them in this wild jungle, is there?"

"Mr. Dark—Kellan," she said. "I think—"

The next thing she knew, he'd grabbed her hand and tugged her quickly and firmly from the doorway, and in the same movement, he closed the bamboo door behind her.

"Mr. Darkdale!" she exclaimed, yanking from his grip. Her shawl was on the floor and her breasts threatened to erupt from the confines of their stays as she fought to control her breath. "What are you doing?"

"Miss Clemons…Jane…forgive me," he said. "I didn't mean to frighten you—"

"I'm not frightened of you. But you must leave, now," she said, and realized with horror that one of her nipples was showing. Her breast had popped out from the corset and chemise during her sudden movements, and now it sat there, round and full and pink-tipped, right where they both could see it.

They both looked down and the room went silent and tight.

"Oh, Jane," Kellan said, his voice rough and pained, his eyes fastened on her breast. "Do you have any idea how badly I want you? All this long trip, all those days aboard the ship....I know you loved Jonathan, but he's gone. And I'm here. And... Jane, I know how much you must miss him...and the touch of a man. I know what a passionate woman you are."

"Kellan," she said, hardly able to wonder how he knew such a thing. Surely Jonathan hadn't—

Suddenly he was there, pulling her into his arms.

"Jane," he groaned again. His mouth fastened over hers, smothering any response she might have made, and his hand covered her bare breast. Jane pushed at him, trying to twist her face from his kiss, but his tongue probed deeply as his desperate teeth cut into the sides of her mouth. He plundered and tasted, his tongue thrusting hard and sleek as his lips sucked and nibbled.

One arm was a strong band around her waist, holding her in place against his body. His other hand found her nipple and pinched it, rolling it between the pads of his fingers. A little jolt of pain arced through her, followed by a sharp, hard twinge of reluctant pleasure, cutting through her dismay. Jane felt the hard ridge of his cock pressing into her thigh, only inches away from the juncture of her own thighs.

She pushed at him, trying to twist away from his greedy mouth. Her heart was pounding with anger and a little bit of fear; surely this was a misunderstanding. It had been the unfortunate sight of her bare breast that had set him off, loosened his control.

But the next thing she knew, the bed was behind her and

his weight bore her down onto the soft mattress. His mouth, thankfully, moved from her lips and she managed, "Mr. Darkdale! This cannot be happening!"

His only response was a deep, low and heartfelt groan as he shifted to take her into his mouth. His warm, wet lips covered a nipple that had been pinched and teased into attention, and when he began to suck on it, Jane felt the sensations shooting through her body, down to her quim: pain battling with hot pleasure for precedence. Her twisting and writhing seemed only to excite him further and his insistent cock pressed harder and harder against her thigh, as if he meant to imprint himself on her.

His hand had found its way between her legs and as she twisted and pushed at him, he somehow slipped it beneath her chemise skirt. Finding that very warm, secret place between her legs, his fingers slid and shifted around, probing and then all at once shoving up deep inside her. Jane gave a soft gasp of surprise laced with dismay and began to struggle with more violence.

"Release me! Mr. Darkdale—Kellan—you must—release—me!" She pounded on his back even as he breathed hard and hot into her neck, his mouth wet against her skin, his hand fumbling between them, down at their waists. Jane knew what was about to happen and she closed her eyes, fighting and twisting as hard and desperately as she could.

All at once, a loud roar—spine-tingling and ferocious—blasted through the night. Jane screamed. Mr. Darkdale bolted up and away from her, stumbling backward, wild and dark-eyed. It sounded as if the feral cry had come from just beyond her window.

"My shotgun!" he exclaimed, looking about frantically as Jane grabbed up a blanket with which to cover herself. "I'll get my shotgun!"

She stared out the window, expecting some bright yellow

eyes and even a snarling mouthful of white teeth to invade her chamber. But there was nothing to see but shadows and the tops of trees filtered with moonlight.

However, Kellan Darkdale meant to take no chances, and he rushed from the chamber, ostensibly to collect his shotgun.

Jane, who at the moment found the possibility of a wild feline in her chamber to be preferable to the presence of Kellan Darkdale, slammed closed the bamboo door behind him and latched it shut with a sturdy piece of bamboo that served as a bolt.

Then, her heart still racing and her neck and breast dripping with his sloppy moisture, she collapsed onto her bed and lay there. Waiting. There were no other noises, no other wild calls. Nor did some ferocious feline leap into her chamber.

A moment later, Mr. Darkdale was back. The door held firmly when he tried to rush through it, and she heard his exclamation of surprise.

"Go away, Mr. Darkdale," Jane told him, wishing the fool hadn't ruined her evening. She sat up and began to unlace her corset with unsteady fingers.

"Miss Clemons...Jane...please...I was overcome. Forgive me. I...I vow it will never happen again."

"It certainly won't," she told him. "The next time you enter my bedchamber, I'll shoot you." She'd already decided to appropriate one of her papa's pistols and keep it hidden under her bedclothes. It seemed as if that would be a most convenient location, based on Darkdale's fondness for that piece of furniture.

"But Jane...there was a tiger or a lion or some creature—"

"I'll take my chances," she told him as her corset loosened enough that she could wriggle out of it. "Now go away."

She closed her eyes and lay back onto her mattress, concentrating on the soft, sweet breeze filtering through the uppermost trees and into her chamber. But her chemise was still a barrier to completely feeling the gentle air and once more she sat up. This time, she tugged the light cotton gown up and over and sat on her bed, completely nude.

The night air beckoned and Jane went to the large window and stood there. She heard the rush of waves in the distance, heard the sounds of wildlife in the night: coos of birds, clicking sounds, rustling noises, and, in the distance, a low, deep animalistic roar.

Her long curling hair feathered with the breeze over her bare skin, and the sensation erased the memory of Darkdale's insistent, urgent touch. Jane closed her eyes and sniffed, smelling sweet, rich floral scents and the tang of ocean.

After a while, she moved to recline on her bed. *I'm going to sleep naked tonight.* She smiled to herself as she lay there, enjoying the sensual breeze over firm nipples, skating lightly over the skin of her belly. Such freedom.

She never had such freedom of sensuality back in London, even in Jonathan's bed.

He was very near the large window, watching the woman with the burning hair. She couldn't see him; he was in the shadows, hidden by thick leaves and vines. Like the big cats, he'd moved noiselessly, making his way from branch to branch to tree to tree until he was just outside the large opening.

If he reached out a finger, he could touch the wall. He sniffed silently, and amid the familiar scents of the jungle—the flowers, the damp soil, the underlying decay of plant and animal, the proximity of a tree monkey—he smelled something new. He smelled *her*. Musky and sweet and exotic. Something he'd never scented before; but an essence that drew him.

He couldn't pull his eyes away as she took off her dress—that was another word he'd learned in the books—and saw all of the roundness there. The jouncing and the curves and the smooth, hairless, ivory skin…and a patch of fire between two legs. He wanted to touch that fire.

His heart was pounding and there were other parts of him pounding too. *Never.* He'd never seen anything he wanted to touch, to smell, to taste so badly.

And he was not the only one who meant to touch the woman. In the darkness, his face turned fierce and he forced back an angry growl. The tall man had tried to touch the woman, to take from her, to mate with him, and she hadn't wanted him to.

She'd fought with him, but the foul man had his hands on her body, his red, wet mouth, his fingers leaving dark marks on her ivory skin. Her face had been frightened and angry, and the foul man's expression had been hungry. Deprived.

Now, he gripped the rough bark of the tree. Though the woman had fought and struck at the foul man, the sight of the two bodies writhing and twisting caused his breathing to change and his face to heat. His veins pounded, blood surging through his body. He didn't want to see the woman hurt, he had to do something…but the images made his insides move. Made them heat and tingle and…want.

And so he helped her. He could mimic the sound of any creature in the jungle, and he chose to growl the most threatening sound he knew: that of a hungry, angry tiger. He smiled to himself in the dark when the foul man had jumped away, stumbling off of the woman, panic and cowardice blazing in his face.

And when the woman closed the door behind him, he knew she was intelligent and strong.

And he wanted even more to touch her.

Unseen and silent, he watched her for a long time as she lay, uncovered, on her bed, in the soft yellow glow of a flame.

He could tell when she fell asleep, for her breathing changed, her body relaxed. Her head turned to one side, her vibrant, burning hair covering a cheek and curling over her neck and shoulder.

Heart pounding, he slid down to the branch on which her nest rested. His fingers curled over the edge of the wall and he sniffed. Hot sensation rushed through him. Her smell was beautiful, and it made him feel almost the way he did when he breathed the smoke burning from the special negaru plant.

He wanted to bury himself in that delicious, compelling scent, his face and nose close to her skin and in the warmest parts of her curves. He closed his eyes for a moment, steadying his breathing. He couldn't make a sound or she might waken.

Then, silent as the tiger he'd mimicked earlier, he climbed into the nest. Heart pounding, he stood next to her pallet, in the shadows and looked down.

Such a thing of beauty. He could hardly breathe. The burning hair lay spread all over her pallet and her white shoulders, down over her belly…almost to the second, smaller, shorter patch. Round white globes, tipped with small pink flowerbuds, rose and fell with her easy breaths.

He tightened his fingers into his palm to keep from touching her.

Suddenly, she shifted in her sleep. He stilled, slowing his rough breathing into silence. She gave a soft moan and a sigh, and as she moved, her hand rose and slid to cover the short, burning patch between her legs.

Her foot shifted and her legs opened, showing a large portion of the pallet between them.

He reminded himself to breathe, to draw in air, for his vision seemed to tilt and sway. He couldn't pull his eyes from her. His body felt hot and engorged and he watched breathlessly as she moved her fingers.

They fluttered between her legs, shifting delicately into the short, burning fur…then they tensed and straightened, and she began to rub herself. It was rhythmic and steady, and it reminded him of the mating movements he'd seen in any number of animals. Her legs shifted helplessly, her head turned from one side to the other and the hair covering her face fell away. Her body arched and relaxed as though she were reaching for something…longing for something.

Her mouth was open and she was making sounds… soft, panting sounds that tugged pleasure deep inside him. Her particular smell grew stronger, more delicious, filling his nostrils and making his clenched fingers tremble. He wanted to taste her…touch his lips to her smooth skin, find the place of that essence and drink.

She moved her other hand, using her fingers to massage the rosy pink tip on one of the soft globes. They moved lightly over the little point, then in small circles around and over it. His keen eyes saw it shudder and tremble when she drew in a deep, long breath.

He noticed the fingers between her legs had become damp and slick, gleaming in the moonlight. Her white hand moved more rapidly and urgently there in the dark shadowy space between and her breathing had become so loud and labored that he might have thought she were in pain if he hadn't been watching for so long.

This was not pain.

It took every bit of fortitude he had—the same strength that had helped him to kill a feral tiger in a hand-to-paw battle, the same control that had kept him alive when he left the ape family that had raised him from a young child—to keep from touching her.

But he inched closer to the place where she lay, watching from the shadows that would obscure him if she opened her eyes. His fingers loosened, wanting to reach for her, and the blood pulsed through his body—hard and fast and *hot*. The leather piece he wore to protect his male parts lifted straight out in front as his rod throbbed and shivered.

He was waiting…waiting…but he didn't know what he

was waiting for. She made a sound that sent a renewed shock of heat and sharp pleasure bolting through him, a soft cry of surprise and need, and then all at once, she gave a low gasp and arched up. Her smell exploded even more strongly, and then she was whimpering and shuddering and shivering.

He knew, somehow, that this was what he'd been waiting for. His rod was so hard it was painful, it dripped moisture from the tip, and he knew if he touched it, it, too would explode.

Her hand, glistening and damp, fell away, relaxing open-palmed on her hip. The beautiful, musky smell rolled off her in waves, and now he could see that part of her between her legs…sleek and dark and beckoning.

He wanted *there*.

He swallowed, forcing himself to look away from that temptation. Her lips were parted and her face turned to the side. Her breathing steadied and slowed.

The pounding of his heart filled his ears as blood rushed to his rod, and he squeezed his eyes closed. Tried to slow, tried to relax.

But he had to touch her.

His hand trembled as he reached out and touched lightly… ever so lightly…to touch that burning mass of hair.

JANE WOKE SLOWLY. Something warm and light filtered over her skin and she smelled sweet, heavy flowers.

Sighing with pleasure, she rolled to the side and opened her eyes to find soft sunlight and a gentle breeze wafting through the open windows. Her long hair was caught beneath her arm and tangled around her shoulders, for she hadn't put it in its customary braid last night. As she breathed in the scents of her new, temporary home, she adjusted, pulling free the long, curling strands of hair.

She couldn't remember ever having slept so soundly, awaking feeling so rested and…sated. Yes, sated was the best word to describe the sense of relaxation, of satisfaction, of warmth and looseness.

Vague images of dreams that, thankfully, hadn't included Kellan Darkdale, buffeted at the corners of her mind. Sensual, warm, hot dreams….

A shadowy figure had been there, watching over her—an angel perhaps? Or perhaps a memory of Jonathan…for she'd dreamt of a firm, light hand smoothing along the length of her hair. A man's hand.

Jane sat up, amazed that she'd slept so soundly and so well after the shocking experience with Kellan, and with her windows uncovered as well. She supposed she was fortunate that none of the jungle creatures had found it necessary to join her or investigate the new addition to their world. Prudence and practicality suggested that she find something with which to cover the windows…but Jane realized she didn't want to block out the jungle.

Here so high in the trees, with the branches and vines and even the songs of birds so close by, she felt so free and comfortable. Even the buzzing of small insects hadn't bothered her. A bit of mosquito netting might be a nice idea, hanging over the windows…but she decided she would not block them otherwise.

There was no one to see her. No one to judge.

Her insides tightened at the thought, and then eased. She was in Madagascar, far from London.

Crawling from her bed, she used the chamberpot and then washed up with a small basin of water and a soft dish of soap. The scent of lilly of the valley meshed with her own, musky, private scent, and when she smelled it on her fingers, for a moment Jane closed her eyes and breathed. The memory of pleasure and release mingled with the hint of sweet, hot dreams washed over her. She smiled.

And then her smile faded. She missed Jonathan.

After standing once more at the window, allowing the warm breeze to slide over her bare skin, teasing her nipples into hard little points, she reluctantly dug through a trunk to find something to wear.

No more long corsets, she decided. Just a short lace-up one that she could fasten herself, and that didn't need to squeeze her so tightly she couldn't breathe. A skirt of light lawn, and a simple white shirtwaist that buttoned down the front.

A short while later, she climbed down the sturdy wooden stairs that led to the main floor of the treehouse. Here was a large living space that had been outfitted like a large parlor and kitchen, all in one, with built-in tables, counters, and shelves.

A wood burning stove sat on a small balcony so that the smoke wouldn't collect inside the walls and ceiling. When Jane entered, she saw that the moveable walls had been pulled aside. This made the space feel as if the floor was a large platform embraced by the massive branches of the tree.

"Good morning," she said, her gaze sliding quickly over Kellan, who sat in shirtsleeves and dark trousers, and to her father. "Did you sleep well, Papa?"

"I don't b'lieve I've ever slept better," he replied between mouthfuls of eggs and sausage. "Don't b'lieve I've ever had a more delicious breakfast," he added with a look at Efremina.

The cook sniffed and clanged the spoon into a pot.

"Enjoy it while it lasts," Kellan said. "The ship won't return with more supplies for weeks, and when these provisions run low, we'll be supplementing them with whatever game I can find in the jungle." His regard settled on Jane, and she felt her cheeks warm. "Good morning, Miss Clemons. I trust you slept well, and uninterrupted?"

"I slept very well," she replied. "And thank you for the reminder," she added. "I've decided it would be best to keep a loaded firearm in my room. Just in case I have unwanted nightly visitors."

Kellan grimaced and he appeared chastised, looking down at the tin cup of coffee he'd been sipping. "I'm certain if an unwanted visitor made its way to your chamber, it was a terrible accident and wasn't meant to be an offense."

She looked at him, but he was studying his drink. "Nevertheless," she said, remembering his pinching, questing fingers with a little shudder, "I'll take one of your pistols, Papa. Just in case."

"Perhaps you'll allow me to teach you how to load and shoot it?" Kellan suggested, standing suddenly. His pale blue eyes were fastened on her once again. "Dr. Clemons?"

"Missy Jane don' need no help wi' that," Efremina said

flatly, her blond hair fairly bristling. "She knows 'ow t'use a pistol just fine. Just ask them squirrels what tried to make off with the bird feed she put on the trees at the country 'ouse." She gave an emphatic nod.

Smothering a smile, Jane looked at her father. "What do you have planned for today, Papa?" she asked as she walked over to retrieve one of the pistols from his supply trunks.

"Mr. Darkdale and I are going to walk along the jungle shoreline. I'm hoping to find an intact example of the glimmer-headed tyra. They like the salt water, but weave their cocoons beneath the bark of the north-side of a tree." Papa hopped to his feet as if remembering what an exciting day he had planned, and Jane watched in fond amusement as he began to organize his tools for the day.

"Very well, Papa. Have a wonderful time."

"And don't you f'get the luncheon packet I got for ya," Efremina said, making it sound like an accusation and foregone conclusion that he would.

"And what do you have planned, Miss Clemons?" asked Kellan. "Would you like to accompany us? Don't you intend to make drawings for the professor?"

"No, thank you," she replied. "I have several trunks to unpack and supplies to organize. There will be other opportunities for me to accompany you, Papa, won't there?"

And, with Kellan Darkdale otherwise occupied accompanying her papa, Jane intended to do a bit of exploring near their camp. It would be unlikely, but there could be a clue to Jonathan's disappearance, even after three years. She was certain she'd find the man she loved—or at least a trace of him.

And, just as compelling of a motivation…she might even find a small pool where she might bathe.

After all, with Papa and Kellan gone, there was no one to see her but a glimmer-headed tyra and perhaps a parrot or two.

Some time later, Jane found herself pushing away thick, heavy green brush as she made her way into the jungle. She hadn't gone far, but she was already warm from the heavy, humid heat. The treehouse loomed behind her, and she used it as a landmark to make certain she didn't wander too far from the relative safety of the small inlet of seashore.

Jane hadn't come unprepared. She carried the loaded pistol, and she had several items tucked into a loose belt: more bullets, matches, a small packet of food, an old-fashioned skin of water, a knife, and *Con Bellingworth's Pictorial of the Madagascar Jungle.* Since convincing Papa she should accompany him on this journey, she'd been studying this treatise so as to familiarize herself with the inhabitants of the African jungle. Despite its title, however, Jane was disappointed with the lack of pictures in the book. There were drawings, but they were often crude and lacked enough detail for her to be certain her identifications were accurate.

She could do a much better job of sketching the flora and fauna than whoever had done this.

Regardless of her studies of the book, she had no intention of going far from the encampment this first day. The last thing she wanted to do was get lost and have to spend the night in the cold, dark jungle filled with feral creatures—as Mr. Bellingworth had done. He'd written about it in great detail.

And, she thought with a pang, it was quite possible the same had happened to Jonathan when he was lost in the jungle. Perhaps she'd find evidence of a camp he'd made, or some of his belongings still intact against the weather. If she could just find a sign of him, *any* sign....

She just hoped it wouldn't be a pile of his bones.

Submerging that horrible, gruesome—yet sobering—thought, Jane continued on and turned her attention toward finding a place to bathe.

She pulled aside a swath of ferns, each leaf of which was

nearly as large as her torso, and stepped on soft, squishy moss. A bird called in the distance, another answered high above her, and something rustled in the leaves. Springing up everywhere were the wrist-thick liana branches, which grew from the ground up into the trees and anchored, vine-like, around them. Mr. Bellingworth indicated they were strong enough to hold the weight of a man, and he'd described seeing monkeys and even orangutans using the lianas to glide from one tree branch to another. She touched a tree trunk and something skittered away beneath her fingers: a flat, gray insect that had been camouflaged by the bark.

At last, Jane heard a soft rumble that sounded like water falling.

Patting the small bag she wore crosswise over her torso, she thought longingly of immersing herself and washing her hair. The bathing opportunities on *The Fledgling* had been limited to hip baths and pouring pail after pail of water over her long hair. She'd nearly been frustrated enough to cut her hair short, but something had held her back.

Hope.

Yes, Jonathan had loved her long curls. And if there was any chance of finding him alive, well…she wanted to be just the way he remembered her.

In her small bag, she optimistically carried a small bar of soap, a comb, and a bit of lavender-scented cornstarch and bicarbonate soda to sprinkle beneath her arms and in her other private places after her bath.

In her impractical skirt, Jane trudged through the thick brush, following the sound of rumbling, gurgling water. The thick, rich scent of loamy soil, damp and filled with nutrients, was pleasant and fresh. The aroma of pink, yellow and orange flowers seemed to carry further and more readily on the soft breezes than that of the roses and lilies in her gardens back home.

Once, something rustled in the leaves and Jane went stock-still. Her hand went to cover the butt of her pistol and her heart stopped beating for a moment. Then a small yellow and black lizard appeared, scuttling along a tree branch that sprang from a thick cluster of leaves. Jane was not a particularly squeamish person, and she reached out to touch the creature's back.

She touched its warm, dry, scaly skin before it skittered off about its business, disappearing into the thick green leaves. And then, ducking beneath a series of low-hanging vines that acted almost like a screen, she found a small circular pool.

In her most exorbitant fantasies, Jane had never imagined such a beautiful place. She paused, overcome by the sheer loveliness of crystal blue water, spilling from the side of a small mountain into a parlor-sized pool below. Water so blue, it would put her sapphire earrings to shame. The rough, stone side of the mountain that rose above was softened by lush green ferns, vines, and leafy bushes. Flowers of every shade of pink to red to salmon to rose grew in abundance in the small glen.

Jane wasted no further time. She pushed past lianas thicker than her wrist and pliable vines as slender as her pinkie, hurrying over springy moss toward the pool as if summoned by some powerful entity: cleanliness and relaxation.

Moments later, after assuring herself there was no evidence of human presence currently in the vicinity, she was barefoot on the soft, warm moss. She unbuttoned her shirtwaist and draped over a bush.

Jane stepped out of her skirt and had a momentary thrill of excitement, wearing only her chemise and a short, relaxed corset in the middle of the jungle.

She looked at the sparkling blue water, frothy as a cream soda where it spilled down into the pool, and drew in a deep breath. Then she unfastened her corset, tossed it aside, and then, at last, whipped the light cotton chemise over her head.

Yanking pins from where they anchored her braid in place,

Jane arranged them in a pile on a smooth rock and shook her long hair free and loose. And then she dipped a curious toe into the pool, busy with waves and surges from the waterfall.

"Ahhh," she moaned aloud. The water was cool and refreshing without being icy-cold.

With one last glance around, a broad, enthusiastic smile on her face, Jane gave a soft laugh and walked into the pool. Only four steps in, and the water was up to her hips.

She dove forward, sliding into the sleek embrace of the warm, churning pool. Her hair fanned about her under the water, creating a red-gold aura that straightened and then coiled up with every rhythmic stroke.

Jane, who'd learned to swim at Bassenthwaite Lake the summer she was ten, had never known how freeing it was to feel completely unencumbered, for of course she'd never swum naked, her breasts free to bounce and sway with the movement of the water, the water cool in the warmth between her legs. The freedom was glorious.

When she surfaced, it was in the midst of the waterfall's spill. She tread water there for a long moment, enjoying the droplets of mist on her skin and feeling the way the water rumbled beneath the surface.

It churned so powerfully that the vibration of the falling stream caused the water to surge around her in strong, insistent vibrations. Jane slid onto her back, floating, paddling herself gently, feet-first into the tumbling, chaotic mess, allowing her knees to relax open.

She gasped aloud, arching in surprise when the rhythmic pounding of the churning water surged against the hot, sensitive lips of her quim. It was a sensation she'd never felt before: strong, yet soft, insistent and pulsing.

Oh…

She closed her eyes, allowing her legs to relax, using delicate movements of her hands to keep her positioned in the fiercest part of the waterfall. The erotic slide of water washed over her breasts, leaving them free and tight under the sunshine… then another rush of water slipped over them like seductive fingertips. Little bumps rose on her skin as the roiling pool pounded against her quim, licking and surging over the sweet little pea that brought her so much pleasure.

Pound, pound, pound….

Jane sighed as the familiar heat of lust swelled inside her, weakening her knees, warming her torso, building and surging into a sudden, long stream of pleasure that had her moaning into the darkness of the jungle.

When she opened her eyes, she realized she'd floated away from the turbulence and was now near the shore near where she'd entered the pool. Her body felt alive and full, warm and sated and she smiled to herself.

She looked up and screamed.

TWO DARK, BEADY EYES STARED at Jane. Beneath them was a long, hairy snout and bared teeth. It seemed to leer at her as it stepped into the pool and smacked its long, hairless tail in the water.

She choked on another scream as she floundered beneath the surface, her idyll shattered as terror galvanized her into movement. Jane hardly knew what she was doing as she slapped and struggled through the water across the pool, getting as far away from the large, hairy, rat-like creature as she could.

She stumbled onto shore and, heedless of her nakedness, ran from the pool and its dog-sized rodent as fast as her trembling legs would allow. Branches and bushes scratched and caught at her, snagging her long hair and twining it around twigs. She yanked at it, pulling with her hands as she tried to free herself and eventually make her way back toward the treehouse…but she realized with a horrified start she could no longer see the landmark.

The trees were too tall and thick, nearly blotting out the sun. Jane broke off a branch, freeing her hair, and thrashed blindly to the right, hoping she'd find her way back to a clearing where she could look up and get her bearings. She pushed through a small space webbed with a tight netting of vines and lianas, shoving them out of the way furiously and with no little desperation.

But as she pushed through them, more looping vines fell and twisted, tangling around her as if they were grasping at her limbs. Jane fought them away, but it was as if she'd stepped into a Cat's Cradle made of gigantic yarn, twining and tangling around her hair and her arms and legs. The more she fought, the more entangled she became until she realized she was truly caught.

Jane stopped moving, trying not to panic, forcing herself into calmness. *This isn't a gigantic spider web*, she told herself. Clearly, these were green vines, the same ones she'd pushed aside and walked through during her trek to the pool. They just happened to be very tangled and thick here, and she'd knotted herself up in them.

No need to panic.

And so she tried to painstakingly loosen her hair, using arms bound by finger-thick vines, standing on legs imprisoned by other, thicker ropes. It was an impossible task: her hair was too thick and long and curly, and it had caught up high and wide in the vines, and she was going to have to call for—

Jane realized she was speaking aloud to herself when all at once, something dropped down in front of her, and she opened her mouth to scream—and realized it was already open.

It was a *man*. He'd jumped down from some great height in the trees and landed no more than ten feet away.

A soft strangled sound came from her throat and Jane thought she might faint. She closed her mouth and willed herself to stay calm even though her heart was beating as if it were about to burst free from her ribcage.

She'd never seen a man who looked like him. He was... wild. Uncivilized.

What was he going to do to her?

He was naked except for what looked like two pieces of animal skin tied around his waist, one each at front and back.

He had brown hair with some lighter streaks as if the sun had touched it. The longest hair she'd ever seen on a man reached past his shoulder blades, and was in odd finger-sized, curl-like ringlets. His skin wasn't as dark as an African's, but was more the color of shelled almonds, and he had a light smattering of darker hair over his chest that narrowed into a slender trail, disappearing beneath the animal skin.

His arms were large and muscular, and he had broad, square shoulders and a torso so firm and sleek it could have been carved from oak. Jonathan certainly hadn't looked so… taut. And tight. Powerful. And this man's legs were massive, muscular, and completely exposed from foot to hip.

Jane swallowed hard, trying to keep her mind from going blank with terror. He was huge, and obviously strong, and she was completely defenseless. She realized she was panting with fear and drew in a deep breath, which only served to remind her how helpless she was. At her movement, the vines swayed from their moorings above, but didn't release her.

She looked at the man, terrified at what she might see in his eyes. They were blue, confirming that he was clearly not a native, and perhaps even of European descent. And instead of wildness or threat, or even lust in them, she saw…curiosity. And…concern?

They looked at each other, neither speaking or moving for a long moment. At last, seeing nothing in his eyes to alarm her, Jane relaxed a little. Her arms, aching now from their unaccustomed work swimming, and then struggling, hung helplessly from where they were caught up in the vines.

She moistened her lips and said, "Please. Help me." And she gestured as well as she could, trussed up like a goose.

He made a noise, soft and gruntlike, and then stepped closer. Jane forced herself to keep from recoiling, expecting the wild man to bring the unwashed stench she'd experienced from being in close quarters with men on *The Fledgling*. But the only thing she smelled was sharp freshness, like grass and leaves and nature, and something that could only be described as *man.*

Her heart pounded so hard she was sure her breasts—oh, God, they were naked and exposed!—were jolting visibly with the rhythm. Try as she might, she couldn't twist to try and hide her private place with a well-positioned thigh, either.

He sniffed, lifting his face like a hound scenting the hunt in the air, and she watched his expression change as he seemed to recognize whatever it was he was smelling. Her? Her soap? Something else? Whatever it was, it turned his eyes darker and his nostrils flared as if wanting to draw in as much as possible.

Jane swallowed and tried to keep herself calm as she read the naked, needy expression in his eyes. "Please," she said again. "Help me."

He seemed so wild and primitive. Would he understand? Was he more man than beast, or would the animalistic side of him win out? She knew there were natives who lived in small villages, deep in the jungle. But he didn't seem to be one of them.

The man reached out and she braced herself, not sure whether to expect greedy, grasping hands like Kellan Darkdale's, or impersonal, efficient ones like Efremina's. But instead of either, he touched her chest, just above her breasts, right below her throat, with his forefinger. He made a low, growling, rusty sound: "Uh-mun."

She didn't move. What was he saying? Was he *claiming* her? Warning her in some native language?

He looked at her, and she could see concentration in his expression. Fierce concentration, and then determination. He touched her again. "Wuh…mun," he said, more clearly this time and with less effort. Then, "Wo…man. *Woman.*"

Jane sagged in relief, then felt a spark of empathy for the man. He was trying to communicate with her. She could see intelligence in his eyes as his mind worked quickly and with determination. For a moment, his expression reminded her of a schoolboy, concentrating on spelling chrysanthemum, or reciting a half-remembered passage from Shakespeare.

Before she could think how to respond, he thumped himself on the chest. "Man."

Yes. You are definitely... man.

The thought popped into her mind with great force. She shivered, not unpleasantly—and wasn't certain why. Then she nodded. "Yes," she said, and tried out a wobbly smile.

"Woman," he said again, the word surprisingly clear and intelligible as he touched her once more. "Man." He touched himself. This time he smiled.

Jane's breath caught as a wholly human, completely *male* expression of pride and arrogance accompanied the grin. Aside from that, it had the effect of turning his long face into a pleasing, handsome one with surprisingly bright teeth and attractive creases at the corners of his eyes.

"Yes," she said, swallowing hard and nodding as she kept her smile in place. "Perhaps now that we have that settled, you'll...er...assist me?" She gestured as much as she was able, trying to draw his attention to the fact that she was still tied up. "All the blood has rushed from my arms, and they're going numb."

The smile faded as he tilted his head to the side, like a bird or dog, cocking an ear as if trying to understand. She saw furrows of concentration in his forehead, and then he winced slightly, as if something had flitted just beyond his grasp.

Jane would have spoken again, but he reached toward her once more. She stilled, holding her breath, as his hand went above her head and she waited for him to loosen her wrist.... but instead, he touched her hair.

With a gentle caress, he smoothed his fingers over one of her imprisoned curls. Then, as if growing more confident, he stroked the whole length of it, sliding the lock between two fingers.

"Fahr," he said. "Fah-er." His brows knitted in concentration as he stared at his fingers caught in her hair. "Fire. *Fire.*"

Jane wasn't certain why the wonder in his voice, and the accomplishment reverberating there, made her feel her own sense of pride for him. And why the deep, rusty sound of his voice made odd fluttery feelings come to life inside her belly.

She sensed this man didn't mean her harm. That he was studying her just as her father studied the delicate tropical butterflies.

Then it occurred to Jane that she, just like the insect specimens in the British Museum, was pinned in place, on display. Imprisoned and vulnerable. Naked.

A wave of apprehension jolted through her with such force that she startled visibly. This seemed to draw the man from whatever reverie he'd been in, apparently mesmerized by her hair. His hand fell from her head to hang at his side once again.

Jane drew in yet another deep breath. She wondered if he would understand this time. "Please," she said once more. "Help me get free." And she pulled more violently at the vines, trying to get him to understand her meaning.

When he looked at her, she kept talking. "You must understand, it's not at all proper for me to be standing here in the all together in front of you. And you're nearly as naked as I am. My reputation would be utterly ruined if anyone back home saw this. Not that it matters to me," she added wryly. "I don't care what Abigail Lincoln or that busybody Denna Yarbrough thinks of me. After all, I was the first lady in our set to wear Bloomers and a bathing dress! And I've even joined the Dress Reform Society—as a charter member."

It was a good thing he didn't understand what she was saying, Jane thought in a moment of absurdity. She probably sounded like an utter fool.

Turning her attention to the man, she realized he was

staring at her again, examining her with his eyes. A whisper of sensation swept over her, raising tiny bumps on her flesh, as if he were brushing his fingers over her skin. Yet he wasn't touching her…merely looking.

But the *look*. The expression in his eyes was something so avid, so dark and deep and *wild*…and yet filled with wonder. Curiosity. Even…awe.

Jane could hardly breathe. She watched him drinking in the sight of her, bit by bit…as if he had forever in which to do so. The weight of his attention and examination was so thorough that she *felt* his gaze as it traced over her…from her right foot, over her ankle and up along her leg, slowing and pausing at the juncture of her thighs as if to bestow a brief caress…and then smoothing over the soft curve of her belly, that pale skin traced with a delicate blue vein…then slowing once again as he stared at her breasts, round and full and nipple-taut….

Her skin prickled, her nipples tightening more under the steady heat of his gaze. She could almost feel the sensation of light fingers brushing over her sensitive flesh, sending warm tingles down her spine, spreading over her torso and *down*….

She struggled to keep her breath steady, but something was happening inside her. Something warm and insistent was unfurling like a long, slow roll of heat.

He moved and made a soft noise deep in his throat… husky and rough, and the very sound made the fluttering and unfurling stronger and faster. Demanding.

Jane realized her lips were parted and her knees and arms were trembling…and that her attention had fastened avidly on the hands that hung at his sides: motionless, large, brown, capable.

Touch me.

She smothered a gasp that was halfway between shock and want. *Good heavens, what am I thinking?*

But Jane couldn't stop staring at his hands. She wanted

them on her, touching her, sliding over her skin, curving under the weight of her breasts…slipping between the full, swollen folds of her quim.

My God, what's wrong with me?

Her skin prickled as these thoughts, these images flooded her mind. She felt hot and trembly and lightheaded. She wanted to close her eyes and hide in shame, she wanted to open them and arch toward him and beg him to touch her…

And then at last, he reached out.

Jane stared at his hand, her breathing growing shallow and fast as his fingers came closer. They were fanned open, and she saw, through the haze of anticipation, that they trembled slightly.

When he touched her, his fingers light and gentle against her belly, a shock of awareness jolted through her. Jane gasped softly, stunned by her violent reaction. Her skin leapt and trembled beneath the skim of his fingertips…but she was so aware, it was as if she could feel the texture of every ridge on the pads of his fingers.

She looked up at him and found his eyes fastened on her face, wary…yet with blazing heat in their depths. Jane couldn't speak. She could only breathe shallowly, trapped by his gaze, as his hand moved over her belly…over the curve of her hip…and then up over the swell of her breast.

His thumb brushed her taut nipple, and then—to her frustration and surprise—his hand, rough and calloused, continued up, brushing over her chest and along her throat. Jane swallowed hard as he used the back of his hand, a softer side, to trace the long, sensitive length of her neck. The warmth of his body emanated, heating her skin across the distance between them. She smelled spice and citrus and some undefinable essence clinging to him. Something she wanted to bury her face in, to inhale and take deep inside her.

As he lifted his arm so he could touch her cheek, she was

faced with a sleek, bulging bicep, a forearm sprinkled with hair and a strong wrist wrapped with a primitive twine bracelet. His palm was warm and his fingers sure as they slid into her hair, gently rubbing a curling lock between them.

By now, she was fairly vibrating, still in the grip of the vines. She felt as if she were alive, awake and aware of her own body as she'd never been before…and yet in the midst of some slow, erotic dream. Her insides were overwhelmed by sensation, fluttering and tickling, hot and pulsing, and her quim lips had begun to swell and moisten. Her arms ached as she pulled against the imprisoning vines, shaking the trees and bushes above her.

"Please," she whispered desperately. *Oh please!*

"Please," he said, his response low and guttural and not at all desperate. His voice was taut and he moved closer to her, reaching out with his other hand.

Jane trembled, hardly able to breathe, as he cupped her face with two large, powerful hands, then slid them down along her neck and over her shoulders. She held her breath, waiting for them to cover her tight, aching nipples…waited for him to slip over their sensitive tips…. But he merely curved his palms beneath her breasts.

Watching closely, he lifted them one at a time, as if measuring their weight, experimenting how they shifted and moved and balanced in his hands. Hardly aware of what she was doing, Jane arched toward him, trying to fill his hands, wanting to push her painful nipples against his palms, to rub them against him and find some pleasure. *Please.*

He made a sound of surprise when she did this, and moved his hands away…down. They traced the curve of her waist and hips, slowly traveling down and up…down and up… sending tickling sensations over her until Jane was shaking with impatience and wanted to scream.

She was hot and wet and swollen and her legs were spread

just enough that she could apply no pressure to her needy quim and the little pea throbbing there.

"Please," he said.

Jane dragged her attention from his tortuous hands and looked at him. Desire blazed in his face. He drew in a long, slow, deep breath, as if attempting to inhale all of her essence in one gulp. His sapphire eyes had gone as dark as a midnight sky, and his mouth was so tight it was white at the corners. The intensity of his expression made her knees give out and she sagged amidst the ropes. He wanted her. Why didn't he *touch* her?

His chest, firm and smooth, rose and fell rapidly, as if he'd been running. There was a slight sheen over his almond-tanned torso and she could see the rise of his cock beneath the front flap of animal skin.

Her mouth went dry when she realized what was there, beneath that covering. How close it was, how short a distance she would have to arch toward him in order to brush against it, to feel its long, hard length against her pounding quim. *Inside* her dripping quim.

She shifted, trying to move, then groaned in frustration when she realized her bonds were too tight and she couldn't reach him.

Her cry must have spurred him into movement, for something changed. The hesitance evaporated and all at once, he was covering her breasts again. But this time, he touched her with purpose…curiosity, intent, desire.

He cupped her breasts, then skated his fingers up and over her nipples. Sliding over the tops of them, he gently pinched and tweaked and, when she moaned in relief and need, he paused. Then, experimentally, he brushed the tip of his finger over the very top of her nipple.

Jane shivered.

He did it again, making little circles there, sending sparks of pleasure darting down through her insides. She arched and trembled, and he began to play with her other nipple in the same way. And while his breathing quickened, he seemed to be more interested in experimentation and examination than indulging in pleasure.

"More," she whispered in frustration, her eyes closing as she tried to capture every bit of pleasure, to claw her way up to where she needed to be. She twisted, undulating, trying to get closer, to touch him, to brush her hot skin against his, to feel pressure where she needed it the most. The swollen heat of her quim was becoming unbearable, little tremors hardly more than a tease of what she wanted.

When his hands moved from her breasts, Jane's eyes flew open in chagrin. *No,* she moaned silently.

But when he knelt at her feet, his hands settling at her waist, his eyes level with her full and throbbing labia, Jane could only whimper and hope.

"Please," she begged, staring down at the top of his head, looking at the soft brown coils of hair, the broad dark shoulders…watching those large hands on her creamy skin.

He didn't seem to hear her. His attention was fixed on the thatch of hair that covered her. Jane curled her fingers into her palms, waiting, desperate, for him to do *something.*

When he at last brushed his hands along the insides of her thighs, she nearly cried out with relief and frustration. She shivered, shifted, tried to bring herself into his touch, trying to get him to understand she wanted…*needed*…to be touched *there.*

He took his time, his hands light and careful on her skin, gently parting her thighs, sliding up to the heat and wet she had for him.

Oh, God, please…. She bucked and arched sharply toward him and finally, *finally*, he touched her there. A light, feathery, slippery caress. She was so hot and swollen that this little bit of pressure sent pleasure shuttling through her, exploding into a hard, sharp orgasm.

Jane jolted and cried out her release. He yanked his hand away as if he'd been burned.

"No," she pleaded, her eyes squeezed tightly in desperation. "*No.* More, *more!*"

"No," he repeated. His voice was hard and tight and there was no longer any warmth from him touching her skin. She was bereft and incomplete and frustrated. "No," he said in a softer, bewildered voice.

Jane opened her eyes. "Please," she said again, holding his gaze from where he looked up at her. She shifted her hips toward him, right at his *mouth*. Oh, God, the thought of his mouth on her hot, swollen quim, drinking in her essence had her trembling and tight and desperate all over again.

Still crouched there, he raised the hand with which he'd touched her, bringing it to his nose. As he smelled her on his glistening fingers, his eyes narrowed in dark pleasure, his nostrils widened like a feral animal. He bared his teeth, dragging in a sharp breath as if fighting some deep urge, and Jane struggled harder.

How could she make him understand? She gave a little cry, twisting and shifting and trying in vain to tear at the vines and free herself.

But he drew himself to his feet, stepping back woodenly, as if he were being dragged off some stage by a large hook. "No," he said.

He said the word, shook his head in negation—but his eyes were hot and avid and she saw the way his fingers were curled tightly into his palms.

Jane squeezed her eyes closed tightly again, then opened them.

She was just about to say something when the man stilled. He lifted his face, sniffing the air, tilting his head as if listening intently. Jane didn't hear anything but the rustle of wind through the leaves, and the soft click of branches as they swayed against each other high above her head.

When he turned his attention back to her, she recognized a different, intent expression. Without hesitation, he moved to one of the large trees from which some of her entangling vines hung. To her surprise, he produced a slender implement—a knife?—and with one stroke, sliced through one of the vines.

All at once, the collection of ropes that imprisoned her loosened and fell to the ground in a messy heap. Jane stared, wondering if it had been chance that he'd selected the correct one…or had this been some sort of trap he'd designed?

Either way, she was about to be free, for the vines were falling away. She'd easily untangle herself and step from them, but before she could do so, the man did something else that surprised her.

He reached up and grabbed a thick liana, and as she watched in open-mouthed astonishment, he began to climb it. One moment he was there, and the next, he was scrambling up into the dark, leafy trees—just as Mr. Bellingworth had imagined it. The last thing she saw was a flash of legs as they swung through the air, high above her head, to a different tree. And then he disappeared into the jungle.

Jane stared up after him for a long moment. Her mouth was dry from panting and gasping, and her arms just now had the sensation tingling back into them. Her knees were still weak and the little pearl tucked in the hood of her swollen quim throbbed with remembered pleasure…and disappointment that it had been so quick and unsatisfying.

Then she heard a shout in the distance.

"Jane?"

Dear God. It was Kellan Darkdale and her father. They were coming toward her.

And she was naked!

But before she could scramble off into the jungle to find her clothes, something *whumphed* down from above, knocking into leaves and dislodging small twigs as it fell. Jane gave a soft exclamation of relief and surprise when it landed on the ground. Her clothing and small satchel.

How had he retrieved it so quickly?

Not that it mattered. She looked up into the branches and vines, but the thick, dark leaves obstructed any view of the wild man. He was gone, she was free from the tangling vines, and she had her clothing.

Jane was safe.

HE WAS IN AGONY. His rod was so tight, so stiff and full and sensitive that he could hardly concentrate on clambering up into the trees, leaping from one branch to another to retrieve the items he'd stashed up there.

He knew the moment he touched himself, there would be a surge of pleasure and pain.

But he ignored the howling of his body long enough to drop the bundle down to her, and to watch as the woman retrieved the strange coverings she wore over her skin. The strange covering…what was it called again? Dess? *Dress.* Yes, that was the word. Her dress.

There was a glimpse of her fire-red hair, the small bright patch hardly visible through the thick branches as she pulled on the dress. And then he waited just long enough to see that the other two men—the short, round one who appeared harmless, and the tall one who'd tried to mate with her last night—appeared. His ears, sharp as a wild dog's, had heard them coming in the distance long before they could have heard him. They were there now, and she was no longer alone.

Though he wanted to, *he* couldn't stay any longer. He'd touched her…*there*, where a thatch of fire-like hair covered her full, slick heat…and she'd cried out, sending him spinning away in shock and confusion. The expression on her face had been one of pleasure...he thought.

But she'd told him, *"No! No more!"*

Those were words he recognized from some long ago memory—words that must be obeyed.

He bared his teeth in a frustrated growl. Last night, the foul man in the nest with the woman hadn't obeyed, and from his perch in the trees, he'd seen the expression of fear and anger on her face. He didn't want to see her look at *him* in that way. Ever.

The pounding of his rod had eased slightly and so he gripped a wrist-thick vine and launched himself from the branch on which he stood. He swung in a smooth arc, brushing past leaves and flowers to another sturdy vine. Gliding through the air among the birds and butterflies, he transferred his hold from vine to vine to vine as easily as he walked, as if he were swimming through the air.

Silently and smoothly, he made his way thus back to his own nest where he could tend to himself in private.

There had been many times before when his rod had acted so—stiffening and throbbing. Often, those times were accompanied by vague, hot images in the night. Once, far from here on one of his explorations, he'd seen a group of women with skin dark as the soil, swimming in a stream. They wore no coverings and he'd watched them for a long time, fascinated and intrigued by the shape and movement of their bodies. He saw very few men or women animals like himself, and never any with skin as light as his own. They were the same, but different.

There was only one time before when he'd seen men who came in the big nests—ships; they were called *ships*—that floated on the sea. Men who seemed familiar to him just as the woman and her companions did. The way they talked and the way they dressed....there was something he recognized, something comfortable about them.

But when he tried to remember, to put words to objects,

to *understand* of what they spoke, his head hurt and he felt ill and confused.

That was a different pain than what he felt now, when all of his thoughts, every part of his body seemed concentrated in one place: the thick, purple-red rod thrusting from beneath its protective covering.

As he moved aside the heavy brush hiding the entrance of the cave he used for a nest, he also stripped away the flap of antelope hide he wore. The mere brush of his fingers over the swollen, turgid flesh beneath made him groan aloud.

But now, he was safe and private and alone, and he could allow his body to react. He closed his fingers around the shaft, moved them once, and immediately lost control. Everything surged to that place, hot and hard and fast, and he cried out as it exploded.

His powerful knees went weak and he sank to the ground, onto the pile of tiger and cheetah skins he used for a pallet. His heart was pounding, his flesh was hot and clammy, and he felt better…almost.

But it had been too quick and fast, and his rod, it appeared, wasn't satisfied. It persisted, stiff and insistent.

She'd been the most beautiful, compelling creature he'd ever caught in his trap of made of vines. As he lay here, feeling the softness of fur against his arm and torso, he was reminded of her skin. So soft, so warm, so different from his own, from any animal or living creature he'd ever touched. Soft, with a delicate dusting of hair, like the palm-sized petals of the curling pink flowers he had named lyseta…but her skin was alive and supple.

And the scent of her. He closed his eyes, drawing in the imagined essence once more…then he remembered, and lifted his hand to his nose. A tremor rippled through him when he smelled her on his hand, her scent mingling with that of his own.

Assaulted by the memories, the sensations, the smells, he sank into the images, sliding back into them in his mind, letting them fill his thoughts. His rod pounded once again, hot and hard and insistent.

Closing his hand around it, he did as he'd done in the past—he stroked, faster and faster, his fingers tighter and tighter around the throbbing shaft. Sticky moisture dripped from the tip, making his movements sleek and slippery and fast. He imagined his rod pressed against the woman's warm, soft skin, sliding in the rich dampness between her legs, slipping into her tight, dark depths.

He cried out in triumph as pleasure and release bolted through him, hard and fast and deep. It went on for a long time, and when it was finished, his body still pulsing and throbbing, he slept.

And dreamt.

DID YOU FIND the glimmer-headed tyra today, Papa?" Jane asked her father.

They'd just finished a dinner of baked fish and plantains and were sitting in the treehouse. Efremina had slid the movable wall away, leaving one side of the living space open to the view of the jungle from tree-height.

It was the most unique, comfortable parlor Jane had ever been in. Large, leafy branches spilled into the room. Birds, butterflies, and other winged insects flitted about just beyond reach. The scent of rich, sweet flowers filled the air. The sun was setting, coloring the sky with violent red and orange flames.

"We had no luck finding the tyra," Jane's father replied, puffing on a long, slender pipe. "But I did capture the perfect specimen of a red-beaded long-twine. Perhaps you'll make a sketch for me tonight, love?"

"Of course," she told him, and rose to retrieve her sketching tools. Since Jonathan disappeared, she'd hardly used her pencils and pastels. But it had been part of the arrangement with Papa—she was able to convince him that she should accompany him on this trip because he needed an artist to document his discoveries in pictures.

They could take photographs, of course, but not only did that require a large amount of equipment that took up much space, but setting up a darkroom would have been impractical in the jungle.

Unfortunately for Jane, the very act of drawing only served to remind her of Jonathan. More than once they'd joked that, after they were a married couple, they could travel the world together. He would write the travelogue, and she could sketch the images that would go with it. They would partner to create a book.

Now, Jane pulled out a thick sketchpad and her wooden box of pastels and settled to draw a picture of the long-twine. Her papa had pinned the poor butterfly to a small, thin wooden tile. As she looked at its flamboyant red and yellow wings spread helplessly, Jane couldn't help recall her own imprisonment this afternoon.

Her belly did a little flip and a sudden rush of heat and pleasure rushed through her. Her nipples tightened at the memory of *him*—whoever he was—touching her with those large, dark hands. Despite the roughness on the pads of his fingers, his caress had been tender and tentative...and maddening. Maddening, because she'd craved more.

Her cheeks burned now as she remembered how she'd shuddered and cried out in front of that wild man, that strange wild man. How she'd wanted him to touch her—the naked, native, half-animal man. How she'd wanted him to *bury* himself in her. With a start, Jane realized her mouth was dry and her breathing had gone shallow.

What was wrong with her? How could she even *contemplate* such a thing?

Especially when, only last night, she'd firmly rejected—even fought off—a gentleman who sat here in this very room with her. He'd done nothing more than the wild man had done in the jungle—notice her bare breasts, and attempt to touch her. Albeit a bit more insistently than the wild man....

But today, she'd been fairly begging a stranger to make love to her. A stranger, who, as it happened, seemed to have no idea of her desires.

Thank fortune.

The red pastel she'd been using snapped in half, leaving an ugly stroke of red on the paper. Jane sighed in frustration as she rubbed a matching smear off her hand. Her drawing was ruined. She'd have to begin again.

"Miss Clemons, perhaps you'd care to walk out with me for a moment," said Kellan as his shadow fell across her paper. "I want to make one last circuit around the camp before night to ensure everything is secure. You appear distracted…perhaps a bit of air might clear your mind."

"Far as I can tell, we got plenty o' air up here," Efremina sniffed. "We're missing an entire wall."

Jane hid a grin. Her first instinct was to decline Darkdale's invitation. She wasn't certain she wanted to be anywhere alone with him.

But that was foolish. Other than last night's misstep, he'd been nothing but proper and gentlemanly toward her. And if she was so desirous of male companionship that she was begging a stranger to take her—

Jane coldly stopped that thought. The only male companionship she really wanted was Jonathan.

But Jonathan wasn't coming back. She'd been foolish to even entertain that possibility. He'd disappeared in this jungle and surely had been dead for years now. She'd seen how thick and dark the terrain was. There was no hope of finding any sign of him now, three years later, in such a place.

Jane looked up at Kellan. Perhaps she ought to walk out with him. After all, they were going to be here together for several more weeks. He clearly had some feelings for her, and he'd been sincerely apologetic this morning.

Aside from that, they were going to be residing together, relying on one another. Holding a grudge or creating a division between them would only cause awkwardness and perhaps jeopardize the safety of any or all of them.

She could give him another chance.

Besides, it was a much better solution than fantasizing about a wild man of the jungle who lived among the animals, and probably acted like them too. She shivered and felt hot all over again. This spurred her to action—a movement designed to banish the sordid images of the wild man.

"Very well, Mr. Darkdale," she said, setting her sketching materials aside. "I do believe a walk is just what I need."

If Jane was concerned about her father's reaction to her walking out unchaperoned with a man, she needn't have been. Professor Clemons had his nose deep in a book and a pen in hand as he scratched notes about some winged creature or other.

Efremina was a different story. She looked at Jane with an arched brow, sniffing with unconcealed disapproval. "Best watch for snakes, miss," she told her. "I hear lots of'em, in all sizes—especially the bitty ones—come out at night." She slanted a look at Darkdale.

"Miss Clemons has nothing to worry about," Kellan told the housekeeper in a soothing voice. "I'll be with her." He disappeared down the rope ladder.

"As if *that* makes me feel any better," Efremina muttered. "Yer sure you don' want to take a pistol with you, Janie?" Her eyes were piercing.

"I'm certain I'll be fine, darling. I'll be just a short distance away, on the ground."

Jane smiled and stepped onto the lift. It was just large enough for one person at a time, with walls that reached only to waist-height. It was slower than climbing a ladder, but more practical when one was bringing large items up into the tree—or when one was wearing a skirt and didn't care to give the person climbing down the ladder below a clear view of one's knickers.

Once on the ground, Kellan gallantly used the pulley to lower the lift, and when Jane reached the bottom, he helped her alight from the small platform.

"I'm so pleased you agreed to walk with me," he said.

She noticed he was holding a torch, and the light flickered over his features. He was a handsome man, despite the intensity in his eyes. They were dark and even in the unsteady light, she could see something there that burned intently. She looked away, uncertain what to say.

He unsettled her.

Kellan walked around the perimeter of the clearing below the tree that supported their living quarters, lighting several torches positioned both on the ground and in trees. "The flames will discourage animals from approaching. Most of the nocturnal ones are afraid of light."

Sitting on a large boulder, she watched him. And at the same time, found herself peering up into the trees as if to see the wild man lurking in the branches. Hoping to see him.

And then she felt foolish and hot all over again and forced herself to stop doing so.

"I must ask you about the last time you saw Jonathan," she said when Kellan finished his circuit and approached.

She heard his sigh as he came closer and knew he thought her mission was a vain one—a realization she was beginning to accept. Yet, the stubborn part of her wouldn't completely release the hope.

He offered her his arm. "Walk with me and I'll tell you whatever you want to know," he said.

Jane stood and slipped her fingers through the crook of his elbow. She wasn't certain why her heart was beating hard, and why her insides felt a little queasy. He was being a perfect gentleman. He was handsome. He didn't smell funny.

"When you and Jonathan were here before, you didn't stay

in the treehouse. You lived on the ship?" she asked. "And where did you come onto the land?"

"As you saw when we made landfall yesterday, the sea's inlet here is deep enough for the ship to come very close to shore—just about where we disembarked yesterday. This made it convenient for us to sleep on the vessel each night and disembark every morning. But there were some nights when we knew we wouldn't be able to travel as far as we wanted to go and get back to the ship in one day, so we brought hammocks and slept in the trees on those nights."

"Tell me again, exactly what happened on the day Jonathan disappeared," she pressed.

"Jane, darling, why do you want to relive such a—?"

"Tell me," she insisted. "Now that I'm here, I want to understand what happened to him. And if there's any chance of finding him…." Her voice trailed off.

"Jane, he's dead. No man could have survived in this jungle alone—"

"Mr. Bellingworth did! And there are native peoples who live here—"

"Who are cutthroat and savage!" Kellan told her flatly. "They hunt heads and sacrifice humans, and there are tales of a tribe led by a brutal woman taller than the tallest of men." The muscles of his arm had tensed as his voice rose, but now they relaxed. "I'm sorry, Jane. I don't mean to frighten—"

"Did you see any of those natives while you were here?"

"We encountered no one."

"What happened that day?" she asked again, choosing not to mention that his warnings about the native people were based on tall tale and legend, and stories didn't frighten her at all.

"We came onshore as usual. Jonathan had been studying a map from a different angle the night before and he wanted to try out a new theory he had for following the diagram. This entailed following a northeasterly path—"

"That way?" Jane asked, pointing in what she thought was the proper direction. *A map?*

"Why, yes," Kellan replied. "You can't see it from here, in the dark, but there is a small mountain range that followed a river. We climbed through one of the small passes and then Jonathan accidentally dropped one of the knapsacks down a rocky hill. It had many of our provisions in it, including ammunition for the rifle, and so he had to take the risk of climbing down after it. He never returned. I looked for him, called after him, and he never responded. I went back to the ship and brought the crew to search. We never found a trace of him."

"What were you searching for?" Jane asked. "You referred to a map. What was on it?"

Jonathan had never mentioned a map...."Why did you and Jonathan really come here?" she asked Kellan again. "It wasn't just for an adventure, was it?"

His arm moved beneath her fingers again, his muscle tense. "Surely he told you."

"Please tell me why."

He stopped, turning to look down at her. "It was diamonds. We were looking for diamonds."

"Diamonds?"

He nodded. "Jonathan acquired a map that was supposed to lead to a hidden vein of diamonds. The natives find no value in the stones and so anything we discovered was for the taking."

Jane couldn't have been more surprised at his response. She'd never had any idea of this. "You never found the mine? Whatever happened to the map?"

"No, Jonathan disappeared before we were able to find the cache. The map was old and many of the landmarks had changed. We spent days traipsing through the jungle trying to follow the clues on the map, but we never did."

Jane stopped and turned to look at him. He would have

kept walking if her fingers hadn't been around his arm, tugging him to a halt. "What happened to the map?"

"It was with Jonathan when he disappeared." He was looking at something in the shadows and Jane's gaze followed his line of sight.

"What is it?" she asked, edging closer to him. Her heart was pounding. It was one thing to walk through the jungle during the day…but at night, the wild, feral creatures came out.

"I thought I saw something," he said, his arm moving nearer to his side. This had the effect of pulling her closer against him, and for the moment, Jane was comforted by the warm solidness of his body.

She waited, still and silent, as he stared into the darkness. At last, he shifted, moving his arm so that her grip fell away. "Whatever it was, it's gone," he said.

She would have stepped away, but Kellan reached for her.

"Jane," he said. There was that note in his voice…that intense, almost desperate tone. His fingers curved around her arms before she could step back, and he looked down at her in the flickering light of the torches.

She opened her mouth to speak, to somehow ward him off, but before she could do so, his face descended and his lips covered hers.

Jane's initial reaction was to shove him away, but she stopped herself and forced her eyes to close and her curling fingers to relax. She allowed him to kiss her, in part because she was curious, and in part because she knew her body craved the touch of a man.

Kellan's mouth was warm and sleek, and although she felt the barest flutter of response, Jane felt nothing like the rush of sensations she'd experienced at the touch of the wild man.

When she could stand it no longer, she twisted her face firmly away from his lips and planted her hands on his chest to hold him at bay. His torso rose and fell rapidly, and she saw the desire in his eyes. His lips were full and glistening and his hands tight around her arms. Too tight. A flicker of revulsion trembled through her.

"It's time for me to return," Jane said, keeping her voice steady and calm. "Efremina will be worried," she added, suddenly wishing her maid would holler down from the treehouse and call her inside.

Kellan licked his lips, and the very sight put Jane in mind of an animal contemplating its prey…in an unflattering manner. "I want you, Jane," he said, his grip still tight. "You needn't play the innocent maid with me, or the demure girl. Jonathan told me all about you. How passionate you were. All of the things you like. How you need the touch of a man."

Jane froze, her heart thudding in her chest. Jonathan would never speak to anyone about the things that passed between them. Kellan was lying. "Mr. Darkdale," she managed to say. "I don't think this is an appropriate conversation."

"Then let us not talk," he said. "He told me in great detail, Jane…so many stories of you together…and in such great detail that I could hardly sleep at night without dreaming of you. Without imagining us together, me pleasuring you, sliding between your sleek—"

"Stop!" Galvanized by his disturbing words, she yanked away and stumbled back. "I'm not certain what Jonathan told you, but I no longer wish to finish this conversation. Good night, Mr. Darkdale." She spun toward the treehouse ladder.

"I would make you scream with pleasure," he said, his voice low and tinged with anger, his words wafting behind her as she clambered up the ladder. "Jane, I will taste you. I will have you. And you'll beg me for more."

VII

JANE CLIMBED UP THE LADDER and into the parlor. When her head emerged from the entrance in the floor, she found Efremina holding a cup of tea and watching her. Her gaze was all-too-knowing and Jane's cheeks turned warm.

"See any snakes down there, Miss Jane?" Efremina asked as she lifted the cup to drink.

"No," Jane replied brightly. "Not at all."

The last thing she wanted was for the maid to know what had transpired between her and Kellan. Who knew what Efremina would do (a variety of possibilities had already crossed Jane's mind as she climbed up the ladder, for Efremina had stiff morals, little patience, and surprising strength). And as Jane had concluded, it was important that Kellan Darkdale remain in their camp. At least until *The Fledgling* returned. They needed him, his expertise, and his strength.

"Some of'em snakes can be right vicious," Efremina told her. "They seem harmless and pretty, with their bright colorin', but those're the ones to watch out fer. Those're the ones who sneak up on ye in the night, slippin' b'neath yer covers and—"

"I'm exhausted," Jane interrupted, trying not to think about any form of snake slipping beneath her covers. "I'm going to go to bed now, Effie, darling."

The older woman looked at her and gave an understanding

nod. "I'll be making certain no snakes bother ye the rest of the night, missy."

"Good night, Papa," Jane said. As far as she could tell, Professor Clemons hadn't moved except to turn the page of his book since she'd left for her walk.

"Mmm? Oh, hm, yes, a cup of tea would be most welcome, Effie," he said vaguely.

The two women exchanged amused glances, and just as Jane heard the creak of the lift rising—presumably with Kellan inside—she slipped from the main floor of the treehouse and climbed up to her bedchamber.

After locking the door—which was only a matter of turning a piece of bamboo perpendicular to the door frame—Jane took off her skirt and shirtwaist and used a pitcher of water and its basin to wash up.

Although her bath in the pool had been interrupted earlier (she meant to look in Bellingworth's book to determine which creature had startled her), Jane had finished her ablutions once back at the treehouse by taking advantage of a tub of water Efremina had filled with spring water. It wasn't as pleasurable as swimming in the churning pool, but she'd at least been able to wash. Her hair still smelled of lavender and lily, and as she took it out of its pins, the scent wafted anew into the air.

With a sigh of relief, she unhooked her corset and it fell away, leaving her dressed only in the loose, light chemise. She picked up the hem, ready to lift the garment up and off.

For some reason, she glanced toward the open window. Leaves swayed gently in the breeze, dancing against the bamboo and timber frame of her chamber. A variety of animal sounds—coos, caws, cries, growls—sang in the night. Rustling sounds told her that something moved nearby. A bird. A rodent. A monkey.

A man.

Was he out there somewhere?

A little shiver coursed down her spine, ending in a flicker of heat deep inside.

Was the wild man watching her this very moment, from some high perch?

She turned from the window, still undecided about whether to pull off her chemise. Surely he'd disappeared into the depths of the jungle, back to wherever he lived: a cave, a tree, some sort of crude house….

Who was he?

Where *did* he live?

Had he ever seen Jonathan?

That thought settled in her mind. It seemed obvious that the wild man had been living on his own in the jungle for some time—he was completely uncivilized and could hardly communicate. He must have been away from other humans for years, perhaps even since he was a child.

If Jonathan had somehow managed to survive in the jungle after being "lost," perhaps the wild man had seen him.

Jane looked back out through the window, moving close enough that she could feel the breeze. But it was a vast, dark, dangerous jungle.

She shook her head. It would have been unlikely that the two men crossed paths—if indeed there was a path to cross. Likely…oh, likely, Jonathan had fallen to his death or been otherwise killed when he was separated from Kellan.

She must accept that fact.

Making a decision, she tugged off her chemise and slid beneath the light coverlet on the bed. Then she got back up and pulled down the mosquito netting Efremina had tacked to the top of the window. That would, at least, keep out any small insects.

Jane settled in bed again, all at once very tired after a day filled with such activity. Hiking, swimming, running, struggling….

Pulsing.

Throbbing.

Exploding.

Mmmmm. Aware of the smile curving her lips, Jane closed her eyes and relaxed. The sounds of the night were a wild but soothing rhythm as she slipped into repose.

She must have slept, for all at once she was awake.

A hard, warm body covered hers. Hands grasped her hips, shoving her against the wall. Long, soft hair brushed against her as she opened her eyes to find the wild man there. Against her.

His mouth was everywhere: on her breast, sucking and pulling her nipple taut...on her neck, his tongue sleek as it slid along the length of the sensitive tendon there...then he was covering her mouth, warm and strong and demanding.

"Woman," he groaned.

Jane could hardly breathe, but her body was hot and alive. She felt a cool stone wall against her back, the heat of his body burning into her from the front. His hands held her in place as he devoured her, sucking, kissing, nibbling. Her head sagged back, her knees giving way as heat and pleasure trammeled through her. Her quim burgeoned, swelling and filling, throbbing like a huge organ between her legs.

She tried to grab at him, to slide her hands over his warm, solid muscles, but she couldn't seem to find him, to touch him. Everything was a whirl of heat and wet and dark.

Then he pushed her facedown on the bed, his powerful body settling behind her, pulling her legs apart with firm, measured movements. Her thighs were wet and his fingers slipped through her juices as he spread her wide. He was like an animal, with growls, grumbles and soft keening sounds coming from the back of his throat.

"Man," he grunted, roughly, sharply arranging her with her legs open and her rump lifted. Her face was buried in the mattress, her arms somehow helpless and unmoving on top of the blanket. "Woman. Fuck woman," he growled.

When he rammed inside her, Jane cried out in pleasure and pain. He filled her, deep and thick. Her quim closed tightly around him, wet and welcome, already throbbing with release. He didn't stop, didn't slow. He pounded. He had no mercy, no care as he slammed deep into her, over and over, his hands curled around her breasts, his face in the back of her neck, hot and fierce. He growled in her ear, his sounds like the animal he was, deep and wordless. Feral.

Jane lost herself, her place, her words as pleasure and heat flooded her. She curled her own fingers into the bed, holding tightly as the hot pulsing pleasure rose inside her, filling her high and fast and hard. Her vision was red and dark, her body dripping and swelling everywhere. His hands, his cock...she tightened around him, her body seizing up and at last she shattered....

Awake.

Jane's eyes flew open. She was gasping for air, as if she'd been running. Her blanket was on the floor, and her body was hot and damp *everywhere.*

And she was alone.

Gasping, she stared up at the bamboo rafters, trying to come back to reality, to pull herself from a dream that had been both frightening and compelling. "Oh my God," she breathed, whispering into the darkness, the back of her hand settling over her eyes as she fought for sanity.

She shivered at the memory of the wild man, fucking her savagely in some den-like cave. She'd wanted it. She'd *wanted* it.

Shamed and mortified by her thoughts and the path of her dreams, she shifted, her hand falling away. Her gaze moved toward the window.

He was there.

Jane barely stifled a shriek. She closed her eyes and opened them again…yes. He was there.

He crouched on the edge of the window, holding onto the frame, his knees against his chest. The mosquito net hung uselessly to the side.

The curve of his muscles and the square width of his shoulders were outlined by the silvery celestial light of moon and stars. A soft breeze ruffled his springy curls and danced all the way over to Jane's hot, moist skin. He was positioned such that she could see only a hint of his features: the bare outline of his mouth and the slender length of his nose. One hand curved around the window frame next to him.

Their eyes met and even from the distance, in the faulty light, she read the heat in his. Desire blazed there. His chest was rising and falling just as quickly as hers had been.

Something hot billowed inside her, rushing from her chest up her throat to her cheeks, and down over her belly to the very alive and awake little pearl hooded in its quim. Her heart slammed in her ribcage. She couldn't swallow, her mouth was dry.

"Woman," came a very hoarse whisper from the shadowy figure. His arm moved, sleek and muscular, gesturing toward her. Then his hand shifted, settling back into the shadow of his torso as if pointing to himself. "Man."

Jane was still struggling for breath—a combination of arousal, shock, and mortification. But it took only a moment for her to realize that, surprisingly, she wasn't frightened by his appearance—nor did she feel threatened as she had done with Kellan Darkdale.

She licked her lips nervously. She knew what she wanted. *Oh, dare I?* His gaze held hers and she felt anticipation pounding through her in time with her heart pounding.

Her fingers trembling, she raised her hand toward him. "Man," she said, and then gestured. "Come."

If she'd expected him to leap from the window and launch himself ravenously upon her, she was bound to be surprised. For a moment, he didn't move, and she thought perhaps he didn't understand.

But he'd stilled, as if holding his breath. The chamber became very quiet. Expectant. As if something sparked or sizzled.

At last, he climbed from his perch on the window, smoothly and gracefully, into the room, bringing with him a faint essence of spice and freshness. He stood for a moment, looking down at her pale body sprawled among twisted, rumpled sheets. Her hair was plastered to her damp skin like the vines that had entrapped her earlier. She heard his breathing shift, as if he allowed himself to draw in a deep breath at last, and she felt, rather than saw, him inhale her essence, sniffing, as a wild cat would do when scenting its prey.

His prey.

A little shiver skittered over Jane's belly and arms, lifting the hair there in expectation and anticipation. She swallowed hard, her mouth dry.

He knelt next to the bed, and she suddenly realized she wanted to sit up; she *should* sit up, take on a position of control—

But he raised his hand and, palm flat, fingers wide, he gently but firmly pressed her back down.

Jane knew he could feel her heart pounding beneath his hand, and her chest rising and falling. She had no illusions about this at least. Surely he could read her emotions, just as an animal could read the fear and apprehension in its prey.

The wild man's hand slid down over the valley between her breasts, his fingers just brushing an aching nipple, then skimmed over her belly. Her skin shuddered and leapt, tightening and trembling at the light, warm touch that moved down, down...closer to where she ached and throbbed.

Jane smothered a groan, biting her lip as his hand slipped down over her mound and then into the full, slick wetness of her quim. She struggled not to cry out as his fingers slid over her hot, sensitive lips, making soft, sticky wet sounds that cried of her arousal.

His touch was light, too light, as if he were exploring tentatively. Jane shifted impatiently, and immediately he pulled back, rearing away onto his haunches like a pet being corrected.

She moaned in frustration and reached out, snatching his hand and bringing it firmly, sharply, to her quim. His wrist was wide and warm, and his fingers, long and slender. She curled her hand around his, showing him how to touch her, how to move sleekly through the folds of her hot, juicy labia. Stroke, slip, slide, rub…*rub*….

It didn't take long for him to learn how to tease and tickle, playing with her little tight pearl and fingering her swollen opening. When he slipped a digit deep inside, Jane arched in surprise and pleasure, biting her lip to keep from crying out.

He paused for a moment, but she lifted her hips and he understood, plunging his finger in deeper, up to the knuckle, sliding right along beneath the sensitive hood of her little pearl. She shifted and moved, riding him, reaching for his arm to hold onto, wondering where his cock was…wanting to feel and touch him somehow in the blaze of red heat that had her writhing and shuddering against him. She found his shoulders, wide and muscular, damp and warm, clutching them. He tightened beneath her touch, his muscles bunching and shifting as she pulled him closer…holding on for dear life. Her tiny pearl was ready, hard and exposed, bumping against his hand, and she ground against him, panting, gasping for release. *Please, oh please, ohplease….*

When he drew away his hand before she finished, Jane wanted to scream…but her cry was choked off when he planted his hands on her thighs and held her in place. Open.

Her fingers fell away from his shoulders as he bent his head toward her.

She heard his breathing change—become faster and deeper—and she held her own breath, waiting. Her quim seemed to fill and swell, her tiny pea expanding in anticipation and need. She felt him draw in a breath, inhale her, and the image excited her. His fingers closed tighter over her thighs as if to anchor them there.

Jane shuddered in frustration and shifted, trying to lift her hips and quim closer to him. When at last something touched her there—quick as lightning, hot and sleek—she had to stuff a fist into her mouth to keep from crying out. *Yes!* She pulsed and throbbed harder, hotter, and again he swiped out tentatively with his tongue…just quick enough to set her to quivering, but leaving her raw and sensitive and crying.

"Please," she moaned behind her hand, her eyes squeezed shut, her hips thrusting up as much as his grip would allow. "Man…fuck…woman."

He stilled for a moment, but didn't, as she'd hoped, pull away and shove himself inside her. No, he paused, as if trying to understand her, then, as if comprehending that whatever she meant to say, she wasn't warning him off, he bent back to her again. This time, his tongue was wide and thick, swiping and teasing and lapping at her juices as her quim surged and filled.

His strokes were slow, maddeningly slow, *tortuously* slow, as if he meant to explore and memorize every fold and crevice of her…and yet Jane had never felt such intense pleasure as she felt herself burgeoning red and hot and desperate. She twisted and bucked, writhing and urging herself as he held her in place, tasting and sucking on her ready, full flesh.

"Oh," she cried into her fist as she suddenly found the peak, arching and coiling up and over into a hot, loud, splintering orgasm. *Ohhhh.*

She collapsed flat back on the bed, gasping for breath, her

insides full, her quim quivering and pulsing, her limbs weighty and still.

He seemed to understand that he could release her now, that he could slip his light, gentle fingers over the sated, full lips of her quim. She gave a little shudder, sighing softly, and trembled a bit as he trailed his touch along the inside of one of her thighs.

When his touch left her, Jane opened her eyes at last. He knelt next to her bed, close enough for her to see his eyes, dark and blazing with desire and…pride. Such pride that she gave a little shiver at the pure maleness of it.

She sat up and smiled at him…a soft, wavering smile that required hardly any effort, for she was still weak with satiation. "That was lovely," she whispered, and reached out an awkward hand toward him. "Thank you."

Her hand landed on his chest and he stilled, his breath arrested in its lungs. Beneath her palm she felt the strong thudding of his heart, the warm tightness of skin stretched over flat, solid muscle, and the gritty coarseness of hair.

Oh. Jane almost gasped aloud at the sensations. Strength, heat, man. *Man.*

Man fuck woman.

What would it feel like to have this powerful body, this hot, taut, sleek figure sliding over hers, skin to skin, pressing into her….

She swallowed hard, her body already heating and drawing up again in expectation. *Yes.*

He gave a sudden little shudder beneath her hand, expelling his breath in a warm gust of cinnamon. He hadn't moved otherwise except to stare at her like a rabbit caught by its predator.

Hunger shone in his eyes. Blazing and unmistakeable. It made her insides draw up tight again, and a twinge of pleasure pang in her belly.

Jane bit her lip, knowing what she was about to do, and hardly believing it of herself. Only two months ago, she'd been nothing but a proper Victorian lady, trussed up in her corsets and shimmies and petticoats in London.

And now, here she was, a wanton woman seducing a wild man of the jungle.

She shifted her hand on his chest, moving her fingers to point. "Man," she whispered, her voice rough and husky. She used her other hand to point to her chest. "Woman."

He grunted, his breath unsteady, and nodded. As if he didn't trust himself to speak.

Jane smiled in the dark, feeling a little of her own pride and anticipation flooding her. She could feel him fairly quivering, like a dog waiting for permission to seize his treat. She didn't intend to hold him off any longer, but there was comfort knowing that, unlike Kellan, he wasn't about to force himself upon her, no matter how badly he might wish to.

She flattened her hand over his chest once more, feeling his skin leap and shiver beneath her touch.

Just as she was about to reach for him with her other hand, he stiffened and edged back. Surprised, she froze, her heart thudding violently. He lifted his nose, sniffing the air, then tilted his head as if to listen.

Confused and startled, Jane waited...and then she heard it too. A soft sound, like breeze slipping through rushes...a quiet *slither*. It was coming from the direction of the open window, and she turned in time to see a long, slender shadow sliding through.

It was as thick as her arm.

Jane screamed, but the wild man was already moving. He lunged and feinted, drawing the snake's attention to him, leaping away from the bed.

She watched helplessly as he danced about, teasing the snake. Then all at once, he leaped up, grabbed a rafter, and swung above and behind the snake, landing on the ground behind the arm-thick creature. Jane cried out as he dove toward the beast, but the man was fast and sure and he caught the snake behind its head.

Man and beast grappled on the floor, the wild man's hands firmly around the reptile's body. Its tail slapped and whipped, knocking into the table leg and spilling it and it contents in a loud crash.

Jane pulled herself out of her stupor, remembering the pistol she'd commandeered *to ward off snakes.* She dashed across the chamber, narrowly missing being slapped to the floor by the wild, undulating creature. The man held on, and she could see him fighting to subdue the reptile, bit by bit tightening his grip on the beast's throat.

Its movements were slowing, but still powerful, and Jane now had her pistol in hand. Just as she heard sounds from below—shouts, the creaking of a ladder—she positioned herself in front and to the side of the snake's head.

Its eyes blazed furiously at her, bulging from the grip of the wild man, but still glowing with evil and hunger. She was aware of her breathing, faster and frightened, and prayed that her aim would be true.

"Jane!" someone shouted from beyond her door.

She aimed the pistol as close to the snake's head as she dared, looking at the wild man as he struggled to hold it in place, and taking a deep breath, she pulled the trigger.

"Jane! Are you all right in there?" Kellan shouted from beyond the door. He was pounding on it now. "Jane!"

The snake jolted as the bullet went through its head, and collapsed in a long, black river on the floor.

"Jane! *Jane!*"

Her door was rattling in its place, and now Jane could hear her father and Efremina calling after her. She spun uncertainly toward the door, then back to face the man…just in time to see him disappear out the window.

"Jane! Are you all right? Did you shoot something! Jane, answer me!" The door made a soft splintering sound as the bamboo began to give away under Kellan's battering.

Heaving a breath, her knees weak, her hand slick and trembling where it held the pistol, Jane managed to call back, "I'm safe. It was a snake. It's...dead."

There was silence for a moment, and then Efremina's voice came muttering through the night. "And didn't I tell you to beware of them creatures?"

VIII

AFTER ALL OF THE EXCITEMENT the night before—most of which Efremina and her father were unaware of—Jane slept late the next morning.

When she awoke, it was to the sounds of shouting and excitement below. Groggy, half-asleep from a range of hot, sensual dreams, she sat up and looked around her chamber.

The snake was gone. Its massive black body had been heaved out the window by Kellan Darkdale. She'd heard it tumble through the branches and leaves and land with a thud on the ground below. He claimed he had some use for the creature, but Jane hadn't asked what it was.

She suspected, based on Mr. Bellingworth's book, that it might be served to her as a meal at some point, and she thought she'd prefer not to know until after the fact. There was a dark stain of blood on the floor, and the scent of death and violence lingered in the chamber…but beneath it, Jane could smell just a hint of heat and cinnamon and something fresh.

Or perhaps that was merely her wishful thinking.

The sounds from below were growing more urgent, and she knew it was time to rise for the day. But Jane was slow and her knees were weak. Her body still hummed from the ministrations of the wild man and his flexible, sleek tongue last night…and she blushed when she thought of what might have happened if a snake hadn't interrupted them.

Her breath caught when she remembered the sight of him fighting with the powerful, deadly snake: clinging to the thick body, riding it even as its tail lashed out at him, whipping into his skin and limbs. Jane felt a little breathless at the thought of that dark, tanned, muscular body, and the power and strength he must have.

And what it would be like to have it plastered against hers.

She glanced toward the window and pursed her lips. Kellan had told her she must find a way to shutter it at night to keep out unwanted creatures like the snake, but Jane thought she might just take the chance on leaving the chamber accessible.

It would be worth it.

"Jane!"

Now she could hear her name clearly, and with a sigh, she rose from her bed. It sounded urgent and excited, and she supposed it was time to cease being a slugabed.

"You must come down here! You must see this!" cried her papa from below. "Janie!"

"I'm coming!" she called out the window, a bit crossly.

Nevertheless, she dressed as quickly as she could, slapping water on her face and quickly plaiting her tangled hair into a long, serviceable braid. She climbed down the ladder and found herself in an empty parlor and kitchen. Voices still rose from below, and she climbed into the lift (not trusting her weak knees on the ladder) and lowered herself.

"Jane!" Efremina greeted her when she stepped off the lift. Her round face beamed and her eyes sparkled with some great tale. "Lordy! You won't believe it! Look at this! Look who's *here*!"

Jane turned and the whole world tilted and tipped. Her breath stopped. Her chest felt as if an elephant was sitting on it.

A man stood there, near the edge of the clearing. He had shoulder-length, golden-brown hair and a close-cropped beard and mustache. He was dressed in what could only be described as native clothing: skins lashed together in short, loose trousers and a sleeveless tunic-like shirt. His face, arms, and legs were tanned, and he wore crude boots on his feet.

"*Jane,*" he said, reaching out a hand to her. He smiled.

"Jonathan?" The world was still spinning. She took one step toward him and suddenly, everything went dark.

Colette Gale

Dear Reader:

Welcome to the second volume of Miss Jane Clemons's adventures in the jungles of Africa.

If you have already read the first volume, Entwined, *you need not continue with this introductory epistle, but move directly forward to the first chapter. For those who have not read Volume I, please feel free to read on below.*

During the late 19th century, the British indulged in much exploration of Africa, searching not only for gold and gemstones, but also for knowledge of this fascinating Dark Continent.

Professor Everett Clemons, the famous lepidopterist, and his daughter Jane were two of the most famous British citizens to embark on these travels, and although Jane published a book of her drawings and notations about the butterflies her father studied during these trips, there remained little information about her own thoughts and adventures—until now.

Recently, I was fortunate enough to come across an old trunk filled with Professor Clemons's journals and butterfly specimens, and there, within, I also found the treasure of Miss Jane Clemons's personal journals.

Because there were so many volumes of her journals, I have chosen to publish a series of short segments over time in order to make them publicly available as quickly and efficiently as possible.

I do hope you'll indulge my decision to follow the popular form of literature from this era and publish Jane's journals as a serialized collection. And, I must warn you: also in the tradition of the times, each episode ends on a cliffhanger.

The previous volume ended with the most unexpected but happy appearance of Jane's fiancé, Jonathan, who had been lost in the jungle and feared dead for three years.

I hope you find Jane's adventures enlightening, exciting, and titillating as we follow her further adventures as a young woman in the Madagascar jungle.

Colette Gale
January 2012

The Jungle of Madagascar
1890

"THERE, THERE...SHE'S COMING 'round. The poor dear's had a bit of a shock."

Jane Clemons opened her eyes to see the apple-cheeked face of her maid and housekeeper Efremina. The older woman was looking down at her, a damp cloth held in her hand. It was dripping onto Jane's forehead.

Behind Efremina was her father, wearing a rare, concerned expression. Generally, the only time Professor Everett Clemons showed that particular emotion was at the thought of missing out on the breeding period of the green-spangled midget, his favorite butterfly. "How are you feeling, Janie?" he asked, adjusting the glasses on his nose.

To one side of her father and Efremina was a sharp-featured man with dark hair neatly combed into place. He was clean-shaven, dressed in rugged clothing, and wore an oddly discomfited expression. He was Kellan Darkdale, the Clemons' guide and protector here in the jungle.

Jane pulled her attention from him and her gaze bounced away, settling on the fourth person standing around the chaise on which she lay. *Jonathan.* Her long-lost fiancé.

She closed her eyes again, squeezed them tightly, then opened them.

He was still there. It hadn't been a hallucination. Her lips curved in a tremulous smile.

When she'd first seen him, standing in a group with her father and Effie and Kellan, Jane had taken two steps toward him. But the shock had been too much and she'd fainted dead away.

Now, at last she allowed the seed of hope to blossom into joy. His dear, dear face was still familiar although now he wore a close-cropped beard. His countenance was narrower, tanned, and—she frowned, studying him closely—his skin seemed to have some white and red markings on it. Or perhaps it was dirt, near the hairline. His hair was shaggy but hardly longer than his jaw. And he was dressed in clean but ragged shirt and pants.

"Jane," he said, reaching for her hand.

His fingers, warm and calloused, closed over hers and Jane was aware of a peaceful feeling settling over her. Jonathan. At last.

"Let's give the darlings a time alone, now," Efremina commanded. "It's been three years—they surely got something to talk about." She cast a quick glance at Jane. Then, apparently satisfied that all was well, she shooed Kellan and Professor Clemons out of the chamber.

It wasn't precisely a chamber in which Jane reclined, but the largest room of a well-constructed treehouse. Generous sliding walls moved aside to allow welcome breezes to come through the large kitchen and parlor area, and above and below were several other smaller chambers attached by ladders, lifts, or ramps.

No sooner had the others gone than Jane was peppering her lost love with questions. "Where have you been? How did you find us? How did you survive these three years?" And the one she could not speak: *Why did you not return to me?*

"Ah, Jane," he said, settling his rump on the chaise next to her thigh. "Of course you have many questions. It's a long and involved story, but I'll give you the simplified version. But first...." He leaned closer, bringing with him the scent of jungle freshness and some other unidentifiable essence. "I've missed you so."

His lips covered hers, warm and familiar and demanding. Jane felt an instant of hesitation, then closed her eyes and slid into the kiss. This was Jonathan and he was somehow, incredibly, alive. *Still alive.*

His tongue thrust boldly into her mouth, startling Jane with its abrupt invasion. But his kiss was sensual and thorough, and before long, her insides became soft and wavery. Their mouths smashed and slipped together, tongues tangling and teeth nibbling in desperation to make up for their lost time. She found his shoulders, broader than she recalled them being, and pulled him closer, down on top of her on the chaise.

It had been more than three years since she'd felt the hard body of her lover pressed against hers...forever since she'd covered the long, hard length of cock with her hand, feeling its rigid outline beneath the rise of loose trousers. He gasped and shuddered against her, his mouth slipping away from hers when she touched him.

"Oh, yes," he sighed into her ear. His mouth was hot against her neck, and Jane felt the rise of her own pleasure at the thought of him filling her, sliding in and out of her wet quim.

Her eyes still closed, Jane allowed herself to be swept into heat and titillation, her body swelling and moistening, readying for pleasure. She imagined his strong, tanned body poised over hers, his wide, calloused hands gentle on her sensitive breasts. His long, soft ringlets brushing against her skin, and the ridges of his lightly haired, sleekly carved torso pressing into her curves. The hesitance in his touch. The wonder in his gaze.

Man. Woman.

Jane's eyes flew open.

It was Jonathan pressing against her…Jonathan pressuring her hand down over the ready length of his cock, holding it there as she felt its engorged ridge behind his trousers.

But it wasn't Jonathan she'd imagined just then.

Jane sat up abruptly, nearly clocking her fiancé in the chin with the top of her head. *What am I thinking?*

"Here, darling," he said, drawing her by the shoulders and helping her kneel in a position between his legs. "Ahh…yes," he sighed as she loosened the frayed string that tied his trousers together.

His cock sprang free, full and ready, glistening at the tip with a pearl of moisture.

I must stop thinking about…about anyone but Jonathan.

She settled between his thighs, grasping the length of his cock in one hand and balancing herself on the surface where she'd lain recumbent moments earlier. Licking her lips, she bent to him and covered the dark red head, squeezing below it with her hand.

Jonathan stiffened and gave a soft, welcoming gasp as she began to slide him into her mouth, closing her lips tightly around the hot shaft. Her fingers moved down with the rhythm of her mouth, working in tandem as she concentrated on the pulsing cock inside her…and not on the events of the night before.

She could no longer allow herself to think about the events of last night.

Last night…when she'd no longer held any hope that Jonathan might be found, alive or dead. Last night…when the sleek, muscular wild man had slipped into her bedchamber high in the trees…

…and settled his face between *her* legs.

Jane's insides shivered, and the little bud nestled in her quim gave a sharp pulse at the memory of the wild man and his tentative and then very busy tongue, licking and stroking and sucking there in her hottest place.

She sighed into the next slide down Jonathan's cock, imagining the wickedness of the wild man's pointed tongue, darting inside her, jiggling and jimmying against her until she exploded with pleasure. Even now she felt the moisture gathering there, the filling and pulsing as she worked her mouth up and down over the length of hot cock.

Jonathan's breathing changed, and she felt his cock swell against her tongue and lips. His fingers curled into her shoulders, painful and desperate, as he lifted his hips to slam into her mouth. Jane swallowed, trying to keep from gagging as the head of his cock thrust deep into the back of her throat: *bang, bang, bang....*

With one final, violent thrust, he froze and exploded into her mouth, pulsing and trembling inside her. Jane swallowed the warm, salty wad and pulled away. Her lips were full and pounding, her shoulders sore from his fingers, and her quim and its little bud were thick and damp.

"Ahh, Jane," Jonathan sighed, sinking back onto the chaise. "I cannot remember the last time I felt so good." He gave her a crooked smile and beckoned for her to slide up along his body and join him in reclining.

Jane allowed him to settle her against his warm, damp torso and tried not to think about the throbbing between her legs. Efremina and her father would surely return soon.

And there would be *tonight* as well. One of, she hoped, many more to come. She smiled in anticipation against his chest, imagining a long bout of making love amid the embrace of the tree limbs surrounding her bedchamber.

Forcing her attention away from her fantasies of the upcoming evening, Jane focused on more pertinent thoughts.

"What happened to you here three years ago, Jonathan? Kellan told me you'd jumped down a cliff to retrieve a knapsack, and no one could find you afterward."

"Kellan told you all that?" he said with an odd note in his voice. "I hope it didn't cause you to worry overmuch." He arranged one of her fiery red-gold curls around his index finger, tightening it then loosening it in a gentle rhythm.

"Of course I worried," Jane told him, looking at him in surprise. She sat up and looked down at him, her hair slipping from his grasp. "What else should I have done?"

Jonathan's lips quirked into a smile. "That was a silly thing for me to say, wasn't it? I shouldn't have expected anything less from you than to worry over my disappearance. Well, I promised you the short version," he said, his chest rumbling with the deep timbre of his voice. "And here it is. I did jump down after the knapsack. And then instead of trying to climb back up, I foolishly chose to search for a different way out of the narrow ravine into which I'd fallen. I was naive enough to believe I could find a passage through the small mountain, and then I became horribly lost inside a cave. If Kellan and the others from our party called for me, I didn't hear them."

"I hope you weren't lost in the cave too long, darling." Jane couldn't imagine being lost in the dark, cold depths of a stony passage. She gave a little shiver.

"I don't know how long I was there, but I must have become weak from lack of food and water, or else there were poisonous gases. Something caused me to lose consciousness. When I awoke, I was in a village, surrounded by a tribe of dark-skinned, savage-looking natives. I never knew how much time had passed since my leaving Kellan and awakening in the village."

"A village?" Thoughts of the wild man erupted in her mind. Perhaps he was a resident of such a place. Perhaps she'd been right when she wondered if Jonathan had ever met or been seen by the wild man during his years of living in the jungle.

But the wild man was tanned, but not dark-skinned. And he didn't look like a native.

"Yes. And my first impression was that they were savages, for they wore streaks of paint on their faces and arms—red and blue and white. And hardly any proper clothing to speak of. Nothing but palm fronds and animal skins."

"Were you frightened?" she asked, wondering how she would have felt, awakening in an unfamiliar place with strange people who didn't speak her language poking and prodding at her. She'd heard stories about the cannibals of New Guinea, who shrunk the heads of their enemies after capturing them. But they were in Madagascar. Surely there weren't cannibals here.

"I was at first. But it soon became clear that they meant to help me. And that," he said abruptly, "is the short version of my story. I've lived with them for the last three years, waiting and hoping for the sign of a ship that would bring me back to England. And you, my darling Jane."

"And so you saw our ship?" she prompted. "How near is the village where you've been living?"

"A two-day journey through the jungle," he told her. "I saw the ship passing by out in the ocean. And then I saw the spirals of smoke from your camp. They were thick enough that I knew they came not from the ground, but from the height of this treehouse. I was hoping to find white men, but the last thing I ever fathomed was finding you, here, in the jungle. *Jane*," he murmured, drawing her into his arms again. "You've saved me."

She gave a little laugh and pulled away. "How silly," she said. "I haven't saved you. You saved yourself…and it seems as if the people here were the ones who saved you, three years ago."

He smiled. "That is the truth, my darling. The tribe has

been very kind to me over the last three years. They think of me…well, I look much different than they do. My skin is lighter, and my hair is not black, but light brown. I cannot imagine how they would react should they see you, Jane…with your pearl-white skin, blue eyes and hair the color of flames. Surely they would think you a goddess." Jonathan looked at her, once again his mouth curving in a soft smile.

After a moment, Jane looked away, suddenly uncomfortable under his steady regard. He was staring at her as if he'd never seen her before.

But of course he was! He hadn't seen her for three years… and likely thought never to see her again.

"I cannot believe I've found you again," she said, partly to break through her discomfort. It was normal for one to feel odd and a bit awkward after being separated from one's lover for years. Particularly if one believed said lover was dead.

"Miss Jane!" bellowed Efremina from below. As if to announce her imminent presence, she rattled the trapdoor that covered the top of the stairs, then flipped it open with a whoosh.

Jane and Jonathan exchange amused glances. There would be no further opportunity for intimate conversation—or anything else—until later.

AT DINNER THAT NIGHT, Professor Clemons opened one of the few casks of ale he'd brought from London. Jane sipped the single glass she was allotted, enjoying the warmth from both her drink and the tropics.

A gentle breeze fluttered leaves and the more delicate vines hanging just beyond the wall of the treehouse. It brought a heavy, sweet scent from the bright-colored flowers that decorated the trees and branches. Jungle sounds filled the air: the whistles and coos of birds, the rustling of twigs and leaves, the low cries of animals calling in warning…or in mating.

Jane felt warm, mellow and content. She could hardly believe Jonathan had returned; she continued to pinch herself surreptitiously to make certain she wasn't dreaming. Yet, she found herself looking out into the darkling jungle more than once.

Wondering.

Finished with his plate, Jonathan stood, patting his belly in satisfaction. "How I've missed a good English meal," he said with a smile at Efremina. "I haven't had a biscuit or sausage for three years, let alone a flaky-crusted apple pie! I feel as if I've died and made my way to heaven."

"Go on with you now," she said, her cheeks pinkening. "It was lucky we are to have any shortening and fresh apples left.

And with no oven, the only way to bake a pie is to cook it on the stovetop in a pot."

"Well, if you can do such a fine job in these circumstances, I cannot imagine how good your pies must be back home. And thank you, Everett, for celebrating my arrival with one of your precious kegs of ale. It was a welcome refreshment." Jonathan turned his attention to Jane. "Would you like to walk with me? I'd like to show you something."

Jane rose. Although the sliding door was open in the treehouse, it was still warm and sticky. Fresh air, perhaps by the ocean, would be welcome. "Of course, if Efremina doesn't need help cleaning up. Here away from London, we're less formal," she added in explanation.

Her hands, which back in London had only ever been blemished by paint, had acquired other signs of unladylike behavior since her arrival in the jungle. Scratches, rough skin, and even a little bit of a tan since she hadn't worn gloves since leaving England.

"No, Miss Jane, you take a walk with your young man," Efremina said. "I don't mind cleaning up at all. The professor will surely keep me company."

Jane cast a look at her father, who'd hardly eaten two bites of the sausage and biscuits as he examined his latest specimens (although his cup of ale had been refilled several times). The only sort of company Papa would provide was that of taking up space. He'd be utterly unaware of her absence as long as he had his journals and equipment spread out in front of him.

She smiled to herself. In many ways, that could be considered a benefit.

As Jonathan crossed the room to the lift that would take him and Jane to the ground, he glanced at Kellan Darkdale. A measured, meaningful look passed between the two men, but neither of them spoke. Kellan turned to pick up a book and was settling in a chair as Jane followed her fiancé onto the lift.

She wondered what their exchange meant.

To her knowledge, the two men had hardly interacted since Jonathan's arrival, and she was curious as to whether there might be some sort of discord between them. After all, Jonathan could blame Kellan for not looking hard enough to find him when he disappeared three years ago, and Kellan could be upset with his partner for doing such a foolhardy thing as going after his pack and ruining their trip.

On a previous moonlit walk, Kellan had told her about the map that originally brought the two men to this Madagascar jungle. It was a charter that led to a discovered but untapped diamond mine. Whatever had happened to the map, its loss could be a bone of contention between them.

Or perhaps she was being fanciful. She hadn't noticed any tension between them. The two men had been friends and business partners. They'd been so close that Jonathan had, according to Kellan, talked often and in detail about the intimate relationship he'd had with Jane. Kellan had used that information as an attempt to court her…if one could call attempting to seduce her in her bedchamber *courting*.

For that reason, Jane was relieved Jonathan hadn't invited his friend to join them for a walk. She'd never been wholly comfortable with Darkdale and the way he looked at her. Even though he apologized for the incident in her chamber, she still felt self-conscious about what had passed between them.

"I don't know as you have to watch for snakes tonight Miss Jane," Efremina said with a nod. "Not when y'got Mr. Kent with you."

"What a beautiful breeze coming from the ocean," Jane said as she stepped onto the ground a moment later. She slid her hand around Jonathan's arm, suddenly boisterously, deliriously happy to be here with him.

It was a miracle.

"Come, Jane. I'd like to show you something."

A little squiggle of anticipation whipped through her, and Jane smiled up at him. Her gaze went of its own accord up and beyond his head, focusing on the tall dark treetops swaying above them.

Was *he* up there somewhere? Watching from a shadowy perch?

Jane forced herself to look away, back to ground level. Whoever or wherever the wild man was, she had no reason to care any longer. She'd never see him again, and it was just fine with her.

"What is it?" she asked, turning her whole attention onto Jonathan.

"Remember back in London, how after dinner the men and women would separate? The men would go into the study and smoke their cigars and pipes, and drink whiskey and brandy?"

"Of course," she told him with a laugh. "It must seem like forever for you, but I've only been gone from London for three months. Yes, we women were relegated to the parlor with, if we were lucky, a tiny glass of sherry. We'd have to wait until you males were finished with your masculine pursuits, and then you might join us for cards or games."

"I always thought that an absurd tradition," Jonathan told her. "For why would we want to be separated from the women? There are so many more interesting pastimes with the fair gender. I mention this because the native tribe that I've been living with has a completely different tradition after the meals." He looked down at her and she could see the gleam of his teeth in the moonlight.

"And what might that be?" she asked.

"I'm looking forward to showing you."

Her heart pounding in anticipation, Jane allowed him to lead her away from the treehouse and camp, deeper into the jungle. After their brief interlude earlier today, they hadn't had any further opportunity to be alone. Jane ached to have his hands on her.

Moments later, Jonathan brought her to a clearing in the thick jungle. A bed-sized pool glistened in the moonlight, and off to the side was a small glow on the ground. Jane recognized it as smoldering coals and as she stepped closer, she saw that they were enclosed in a shallow stone bowl.

A soft rumble that sounded like a waterfall drew her attention, and she realized it was coming from the pool of water. It rumbled and bubbled like a massive soup pot.

"Hot springs?" she said, thinking of the Roman spa she'd visited in Bath, England. The water there was rusty and green, staining the stone and marble walls red. Here it was a very different, completely natural setting. She waved her hand over the water and felt heat from the steam.

"Yes, my love, this pool is fed by hot springs," Jonathan told her. She turned to see that he'd begun to unbutton his shirt.

Jane's pulse spiked as anticipation and a spark of pleasure darted down through her belly. Not for the first time, she was appreciative that her clothing here in the jungle was much less complicated than what she wore back home. She could undress herself.

A mere week ago, Jane would never have imagined stripping her clothing off anywhere other than in the privacy of her chamber. But since she walked down the gangplank of the ship that brought her here, many things had changed. Two days ago, she wanted to bathe so badly she undressed in the middle of the sunshine and swam beneath a waterfall, reveling in the privacy of the jungle.

As she untied the simple drawstring around her skirt, Jane shivered at the memory of that aborted bath. She had been enjoying the sluice of water over her skin when a large rodent-like creature appeared, startling her, and causing her to flee into the jungle...where she'd been caught in a trap made by the wild man.

He'd freed her, but only after seeing her completely naked, trussed up in a tangle of vines. Jane felt hot all over again, remembering how he'd looked at her…how the mere expression on his face, the heat and desire and wonder had made her body tingle as if he actually touched her.

"Do you need some help, darling?" Jonathan's voice broke into her thoughts.

She looked over to see him tall and lean and completely naked, gilded by the moonlight. He stood near the glowing coals, holding a handful of palm-sized leaves. "No," she told him with a smile, noticing that his cock had begun to swell, jutting out in a gentle arc silhouetted by the low light. "Jungle attire is much easier to remove than what you've been used to."

"Come over here," he said. She stepped out of her skirt and, as she unbuttoned her shirtwaist, Jane made her way to his side.

He laid the leaves over the smoldering coals, blanketing them lightly. Instead of putting the fire out, however, they began to smoke, and their ends curled then burst into flames. A heavy, pungent odor wafted from the burning leaves, sweet and yet bitter.

"Breathe," Jonathan said, and leaned over the shallow bowl filled with smoking leaves. He took Jane's hand and drew her close.

As she inhaled the heavy scent, she became aware of his hands sliding down her arms and torso, reaching around to pluck the last of her blouse buttons. She made no protest as he pulled the remainder of her clothing off, unlacing her simple corset and untying the chemise beneath. That final flimsy garment ended up caught in the delicate branches of a bush, like a cloud of white cotton.

By now, her senses clogged with the sweetly bitter aroma, Jane was feeling both drowsy and very much awake. Her pulse sang through her veins, her knees were weak, and her skin felt as if it had come alive. Jonathan smiled and led her to the bubbling pool, and just as she made to step in, she noticed him peering into the darkness behind her. He made a sharp gesture and she turned to look.

"What is it?" Her heart skipped a beat. A tiger? A snake? The wild man?

"It's nothing to be worried about, darling," he replied, urging her forward. "Come, tell me what you think of the water."

She saw nothing in the jungle behind her, and she trusted Jonathan, so Jane poked a toe into the pool. "It's *hot*," she said, then stuck her foot all the way in. "Ahhhh," she sighed. "It feels…wonderful." She couldn't remember ever being in such warm water—the baths at home were hardly more than tepid, even in the winter.

Despite the heavy humidity of the jungle air, she found the steaming pool's heat welcome. By the time she settled, naked, in the water, Jane's cheeks and throat glistened with perspiration and her face was hot. Her muscles relaxed and she became languorous, half-reclining against a slick rock.

The underwater spray of the hot springs caused the water to rumble and bubble, surging over Jane's skin in little licks of heat. Jonathan hardly stepped into the pool across from her before he reached for her, settling deep in the water.

Jane went into his arms willingly, the hot water rushing over her shoulders and nearly to her chin as she sank lower, fitting into his embrace. Her breasts bobbed in the rumbling water, tossed and caressed by the hot waves. Jonathan kissed her, deep and long, with warm, damp lips and a strong sleek tongue.

She couldn't breathe—it was hot and steamy, their mouths crashing together, his teeth sharp and firm against her lips. He found her hand and closed it around his cock, holding it beneath the water as he sighed against her throat.

Jane curled her fingers tightly, sliding along the length of him, her legs straddling the outside of his thighs. A rough stone scraped her as she knelt, and her quim spreading wide, open to the hot water and its bubbling, surging motion. Jonathan found one of her breasts, his fingers gently pinching the bud of her nipple. Jane sighed with pleasure, feeling the little tugging throb of her tiny clit. She shifted to press into the top of his thigh, rolling her hips as she surged closer.

"Tighter," Jonathan groaned, and she fisted her hand more tightly around his cock, sliding up to the velvety knob at the top. "Faster." She complied, and the water splashed beneath her ministrations.

He found her other breast, flattening a hand over each one then pulling back to play with her nipples. *Yes.*

Her world was steamy and wet, and when she closed her eyes, everything tilted and swirled, everything felt close and hot and full. She smelled Jonathan, his male scent, the sweat clinging to his warm skin, sweet flowers and damp soil. She felt the coarseness of the hair on his legs, scraping against hers. The hard, smooth stones beneath her knees. The heat of his cock, hotter even than the steaming water.

Jane couldn't breathe. She couldn't speak. She felt as if she floated on some hot cloud, and at the same time, she felt heavy and expectant. She rocked and shifted, moving her hips to find a way to join with him. She wanted his cock inside her. She wanted to fill the heat, the length, slamming up into her—

Then all at once, he lifted her at the hips, positioning her over him. With a sharp jerk, he jolted up into her and she cried out at the sudden shock of pleasure.

He was deep inside her, and she wanted to move, fast and hard…but he grasped her tightly by the hips and held her in place. He filled her, throbbed deeply inside her. She was tight around him, quivering with desire, her tiny pearl full and aching....

"Please," she whispered, jolting against him in desperation. The pressure of his body against her sent a short, sharp stab of pleasure deep inside, but it wasn't enough. Her world was a maelstrom... steamy heat, the waves surging over her skin, his thick rod penetrating her, pleasure and need rolling through her lust-fogged brain....

Jonathan held her hips, allowing her to rock gently over him. His breathing was short and harsh against her cheek as she sagged against him, her hair plastering to their bodies. She moaned again, her hands on his shoulders, the entirety of her consciousness focused on the throbbing, insistent pearl between her legs.

Jane hardly realized when two hands reached from behind and covered her breasts. Someone hard and warm pressed against her back, the unmistakable length of a full cock slid along the crevice of her arse.

She tried to peel her eyes open, but her lids were heavy and the pleasure...it was intense and it dragged her deeper into the slow, hot vortex of desire.

Someone pulled her hair out of the way, someone's hands fondled her breasts—rough, callused hands. She was aware of a deep, low groan in her ear, aware of Jonathan's breathing speeding up and his hands pumping her up and over him, lifting and lowering.

Her own passion rose, spiraling faster and harder as Jonathan moved her with greater speed. The heavy hands from behind became harsher, pinching, twisting, kneading...a guttural grunt, hot breath....

Jonathan cried out and jacked his cock up, high and deep, inside her and Jane felt her own body shudder into completion just after. She gasped for air, collapsing against him, hardly aware of the second hard body pressing into her from behind. The hands, probing and grasping and fondling. She didn't even have the strength to open her eyes, to look behind her.

Perhaps it was a dream. Perhaps she imagined it. Perhaps it was the wild man....

She forced her eyes open at last, and found that she was still in a shadowy, steamy, sweet-smelling world. A glow to her right was the shallow stone bowl of burning leaves, settled now on a rock next to the pool. The sweetly bitter scent curled from the coals more strongly than ever and the world spun. Had someone added more leaves?

"And now," Jonathan said, easing her away from him. He glanced over her shoulder as she slipped free of his cock, floating in the water...back into the embrace of two strong arms.

"Ah, Jane," said a familiar voice in her ear. "At last."

Her insides scattered and her limbs were heavy and yet she was able to look over her shoulder. "Kellan," she said. She thought she said. Perhaps she just *thought* it.

"Yes," he said, and his hands slid from her breasts down over her hips. She felt the thrust of his cock brush against her arse once again, the strength of his thighs beneath hers.

"Jonathan," she managed to say, frantically looking around for him. Where was he? Where had he gone? She could hardly focus. Her mind was overwhelmed by the glow of coals...the waft of smoke...the last bit of throbbing in her tiny nub...the tight pull of her nipples.

"Jane," he said. Jonathan. She opened her eyes and he was there, right in front of her. His face was so close she could feel his breath against her skin.

He took her face in his hands and brought her to him, covering her mouth with his. She scrabbled in the water, off-balance, and at last her palms settled against the smooth bottom of the pool.

His lips took hers, his tongue thrusting deep and long into her mouth, and she had no choice but to try to balance on her hands as her legs rose in the water behind her. Kellan moved between her legs, his warm thighs against her, his hands on her hips.

Jane began to breathe harder, smothered against Jonathan's mouth. Her legs were spread, her hips shifting and floating in the churning pool. She couldn't pull away, she wanted to protest...Kellan rose behind her, his hand sliding down to her swollen quim. He found her full labia, touched the sensitive bud hooded therein. She jolted as pleasure and pain speared her. He pushed and stroked and she felt the throbbing return, a tight, sharp lust. Reluctant, bitter, but needy, nevertheless.

She twisted her lips away and gasped, "Jonathan?" It was a question...her mind was foggy...surely he didn't mean....

"Jane, Jane," he said against her lips. "Trust me. You must trust me. Do you love me? Do you trust me?"

But she couldn't respond, for his mouth covered hers again, crushing away any protests. Any arguments.

Her world spun, weighing her down. Hands shifted, grasping her, pulling her legs wider. Hot strong pressure from behind.

"Jon...you gave your word," said someone dark and deep behind her ear.

"You have my blessing," Jonathan muttered against her mouth.

Kellan gripped her arse and all at once she felt his cock, strong and insistent, pressing against....*No!*

She tensed, jerking against the hands gripping her, but they held firm.

"Jane, easy," Jonathan said, releasing her face to grab her arms. "Look at me," he said, his face damp and glistening in the low dusk. His eyes, the glowing coals reflected in them, burned bright as he stared into hers.

Kellan pulled her arse cheeks apart, his fingers strong but not hurtful. The steamy water burned over the tender ribbons of her exposed flesh, and then she felt something slender slide up inside her. Jane gasped and struggled, but the discomfort eased. She felt full and tight, uncomfortable…and yet strangely aroused.

The finger withdrew, accompanied by a guttural sound from Kellan as he shifted behind her once again. Then she felt a different sort of pressure, there, at her tight arse. His hands spread her wide and she felt him pushing against her.

"Jonathan," she breathed as the pressure became stronger… there….Kellan positioned himself at the tiny hole of her arse, his cock easing in…and *in*…and in.

"Jane, relax yourself," Jonathan told her. "Relax."

Now Kellan's fingers curved into the soft flesh of her hips, and she felt the pulse of his cock as it sank deeper, slowly, excruciatingly slowly. Thick. Hard. Insistent. Pain warred with unfamiliar sensation. Jane closed her eyes, horrified and yet… titillated.

In and in…slowly, deeply…and then suddenly he shoved himself against her, sliding completely inside. Jane cried out in shock as much as pain, and tried once again to twist away, but Jonathan was there. His face close to hers, his eyes burning into hers.

"Jane…trust me…it will be good…." He devoured her mouth again, cutting off her breath as Kellan began to move against her. She felt full and uncomfortable, raw and ravaged… but as he picked up rhythm, the discomfort, the strangeness began to ebb into awkward pleasure.

Jonathan was breathing, short and hard, against her, and before she realized what was happening, he pulled her closer to him. Kellan followed, shoving into her from behind as Jonathan eased halfway beneath her in the water. She struggled to steady herself, her knees scraping the bottom of the pool, slipping into a flattened position against Jonathan.

His hard length pressed against her belly, full and ready once again, and for a moment, she thought he meant to shove it inside her as well. Jane cried out at the thought...and at the insidious pleasure unfurling inside her. But instead, Jonathan's cock remained trapped between her belly and him as Kellan shoved and stroked in short, hard thrusts.

The dark, unsettling pleasure rose deep inside her and the hot water leached energy from her. Jane struggled to breathe, but Jonathan had her imprisoned against his lips, his tongue sleek and demanding, smothering her cries...of protest, of pleasure. The closeness of her world pressed down on her, her limbs trembled and felt leaden. She closed her eyes, grateful to sink into a foggy pool of lust as the unfamiliar sensations grew stronger, overtaking her consciousness.

Kellan's rhythm jolted into her from behind, slamming her forward. She felt full and impaled as his cock moved in its tight channel, faster and harder. Jane clung to her fiancé, but could do little to keep herself from being buffeted about like a rag doll. She was hot, she throbbed and shuddered, she was tight and breathless...and that dark pleasure, so different and strong, swelled and swelled, rolling through her until she screamed her release against Jonathan's lips.

The explosion was fierce, Kellan's and her own. Sharp and deep and it dragged her into nothingness...her eyes wouldn't open, her strength gave out, her body collapsed. Jane succumbed to the intensity of the heat...the sweet smoke...the unfamiliar, uncomfortable pleasure that still twitched through her body.

The last thing she remembered was Jonathan, arching sharply against her belly, and his long, deep groan of fulfillment.

NO SOONER HAD MR. DARKDALE left the treehouse parlor than Efremina turned her attention to other matters.

It's about bloody time. Hard to find any bit of privacy in a place like this, filled with comings and goings and snakes and birds and lizardy insects. But Miss Jane was walking with her Mr. Jonathan, and Effie didn't care one whit where that snake named Darkdale was going—as long as it was away. She wouldn't care if he got lost in the jungle and never came back, matter of fact. Good riddance.

To make certain there were no interruptions, she closed the trapdoor and latched it shut. Professor Everett was engrossed with his examination of a purple-headed riser or thrusting-blackheart or some other unlikely-named specimen of butterfly.

Effie grinned to herself. She had plans for her own purple-headed riser.

She began to gather up the last bit of the dinner dishes and brought them to the large bowl for washing. The bowl was a massive shell with a hole drilled in the bottom, and a cork plugging it up when it needed to be kept full. It wouldn't do to have a mess distracting her. Aside from that....

"Oh lands!" she exclaimed as she dumped a very large bowl of water down the front of her. "How clumsy of me!"

Everett actually mumbled something in response, which was rather shocking, considering he hadn't even noticed his daughter leaving for an unchaperoned walk with her fiancé. But Effie wasn't surprised when he didn't look up from his study.

Not for long, Professor. She cackled silently.

She looked down at her loose, shift-like dress, now sopping with dishwater all down the front. Beneath the light white cotton, she wore…nothing. Scandalously, happily, she wore absolutely nothing.

First of all, it was bloody *damned* hot in this blasted jungle. She had perspired through her corset, shift and shirtwaist just walking off the ship's gangplank. And secondly, no one was about to notice her pendulous breasts and generous hips swaying beneath the shapeless tunic when there was a nubile young Jane wandering about, hardly any more properly dressed.

And that was fine with Effie. The last person she wanted looking at her with lust in his eyes was Mr. Darkdale.

But there was one person who could use a little rising of his own purple-headed critter. And now that her tunic was no longer shapeless….

Effie glanced over at her target, who had a small glass of whiskey next to him and a pencil in hand. His glasses were pushed up onto the bridge of his nose as he studied an open book and his own journal, then looked over at a new specimen, mounted on its tiny pinboard. Helpless. Pinned.

She cackled again. Little did he know that the tables were about to turn.

Effie wandered over to where he sat, conscious of the way her shift clung, unmoving, to her breasts. Looking down, she could see the melon-shaped beauties, nipples tight and thrusting through the cloth in unmistakable interest. Her hips and the vee at the juncture of her thighs were perfectly outlined, and she suspected even the dark patch of hair that grew there was visible through the soaked cloth.

"Professor," she said, standing directly in front of him. "Would you care for a hot cuppa?"

He didn't respond immediately; for he was in the midst of writing a sentence. She waited patiently, the water dripping in soft spatters at her feet, until he finished. "Professor," she said again. "I could make something hot for you to drink."

Effie snickered to herself. *Something* hot *for you to* drink. He had no idea.

"Erm..." he mumbled, flipping through a page of the journal, then jotted another note.

She couldn't help but admire the smooth baldness of his head, shining sweetly in the golden lamplight. Her poor, deceased Mr. Heffington had been bald as a babe the day she met him, and since then, Effie didn't cotton to a man with a thick head of hair. It hid too much. You could tell a lot about a man by the shape of his skull, Granny Melton used to say.

"Professor," she murmured, leaning over to reach for the whiskey glass. "Should I refill this for you?"

A drop of water landed in the middle of his journal page. Effie grinned. She couldn't have planned it better.

The drip caused enough of an interruption to penetrate his concentration. He looked up and she saw his eyes fix on her breasts, hanging right there in front of him. Poor dear. He didn't have a chance.

Effie posed a moment longer to make certain he got the message, and then she slowly eased back. She imagined he could see right down the neck of her dress. And now he could see everything else through the outline of her shift.

"Professor?" she said.

To her delight, his attention moved neither to her face, nor back down to his work. It seemed to be fixated precisely where she wanted it.

"Erm..." he mumbled. The tips of his ears had gone pink.

"Something hot for you, Professor?" she asked. And eased a bit closer. Now her thigh was pressing against the arm of his chair…only a breath away from his arm.

"Erm…" Now his cheeks flushed.

She watched his throat move as if he were trying to force something coherent from it. His glasses had slid to the end of his nose, which meant he wasn't using them to focus. No, indeed. He was focusing on something large enough he didn't need to have it magnified.

Although, speaking of large items…. Effie grinned. Her breasts were magnificent, but in her mind, bigger was always better. She narrowed her thoughts and attention toward whatever nestled in the crotch of his pants. The trousers were tight, growing tighter before her eyes. Oh, yes, those short bald men…they rarely disappointed.

"Something smooth and warm, Professor? More whiskey?" she said, and heard how throaty her voice had become. Mmm… indeed. His innocent confusion and the bulge in his trousers had her insides all hot and bothered. Things were starting to get stirred up.

"Erm…hot…or…smooth?" he managed to say. The pencil slipped from his lifeless fingers and rolled to the floor. Effie took that as another good sign.

Now was the time to take charge. Quick as a wink, she whisked the journal and papers from the desk and replaced them with her very fine, very generous arse.

Thus positioned in front of Everett, she leaned forward and removed his glasses. "I don't think you'll be needin' those," she told him. He had delicious looking lips. And that short, prickly mustache was going to be just what she needed when he was diving into her quim.

She shivered with expectation and her nipples tightened. It felt as if her breasts were going to burst from the tight, wet fabric.

"Smooth..." he mumbled. "Or...hot...erm...."

Edging closer, she began to tug at the buttons of his trousers. *Pop. Pop. Pop.* And then....

"Oh my. Ohhh *my. Oh my!*" Effie could hardly breathe. There was the largest, thickest, purplest cock she'd ever seen. Looking right up at her, a sweet pearl drop shining on its tip. Pleasure surged to her nether parts, swelling them up, making them fat and wet with anticipation. Her little tickler, that tiny nub deprived for so long, was hard as a dried pea, ready and waiting.

She wasted no time sliding off the desk, hiking her sticky dress up, and positioning herself on that tower of pleasure. His hands were still curled around the arms of his chair, as if unable to loosen them. But the beads of sweat on his pate, the raspy breathing and his full, parted lips told Effie he was just as hungry as she was.

When she slid down into position, he made a sound of such deep pleasure she nearly came right then. *Patience, Effie.*

"Hot," he gasped. "*Hot.*"

It was awkward, trying to pull off her clinging dress, but she managed it and flung it to the floor with a satisfying *splat.*

Only then did Everett move. As if in a trance, his eyes still focused on her breasts, he released the chair and gathered them up into his hands. Effie sighed, shifting on his cock, her nether lips full and wet. Her generous beauties spilled over his hands like pearl-white melons, her nipples tight and rosy and ready. He fondled her with those skillful, ink-stained fingers, kneading and stroking as she rocked back and forth on him, just enough to get the blood to flowing faster and harder.

She'd waited long enough for this. She wasn't going to rush it.

He rounded up one of her breasts and leaned into it. Effie moaned with pleasure as those full, hot lips closed around her nipple. Lust shot down through her belly, fast and hard. Her tickler throbbed in appreciation. He sucked and licked as she shifted and rocked, fully conscious of the fabric of his trousers and shirt plastering to her bare, damp skin. She felt him shift and swell and bump inside her, and she tightened around him, kissing him with her pussy.

"Hot..." she murmured nonsensically. "Hot...mmmm...."

Everett corralled all of her bosom into his hands, crushing them together, and then he buried his face in her hot cleavage. His tongue slid in and around, circling one nipple at a time, teasing each of them with a sharp, quick flicker, then he buried his mouth in the deep crevice once again.

Effie rolled her hips, grasping the abandoned arms of the chair, circling herself in tiny figure-eights over the thick pole on which she sat. She heard the soft, wet sounds of her quim sucking back against his cock, licking it with her juices, and pulses of pleasure stabbed her down, down, harder, harder. He sagged back, still cupping her breasts as if they were large pillows balancing on his palms, and suddenly his gaze fastened on her: sharp and aware and very, very naughty.

Effie gasped as he pumped up sharply into her, surprising her with the force and suddenness of his thrust. His lips quirked beneath the bristly mustache, pleased and arrogant, and he jammed up hard and fast once again. She thought she'd scream from the intense pleasure of being utterly, completely filled.

And then she was driving down hard onto him, his cock so thick and hot she swore she felt the ridge of every vein, the curve of his head. He met each of her downward strokes with an upward piston of his own, sliding crazily between her swollen lips, thick with juices and tight around him. Her tickler pounded and pulsed along his length and Effie had to tighten her hands on the chair to keep herself steady, he was so fast and hard.

Faster and faster, wet and juicy, hot and soft, they moved together like crazed animals until the white-hot pleasure peaked. Effie slammed down one last time and felt her insides explode, shattering and surging down over his cock in a fresh sluice of wetness. He pumped back up once, twice more, and groaned as he shot up inside her even as she throbbed and shuddered around him.

Panting, Effie opened her eyes after a long moment, hot and slick and a complete pool of satiation. Her legs were ribbony and weak, her skin flushed and warm, her tickler easing into rest as she eased off him. She sighed. Couldn't remember the last time she'd felt so delicious.

She looked down at Everett, who was watching her with what could only be described as a cat-eating-a-canary look. He looked pleased as punch and just as arrogant as a king.

"Well, then," he said, his mustache twitching. "Shall we try for hot *and* smooth next time?"

And before she could reply, he reached for his glasses and replaced them on his nose, turning back to his jumble of papers.

AFTER A TIME, JANE became aware again.

Her body felt heavy and weak. She ached in some places, but it was a soft, dull, sated sort of ache. She didn't think she could lift an arm, let alone raise her head. Her lips throbbed. Her nether parts pulsed. Her nipples felt raw and tight. Even before she opened her eyes, she realized she was lying on the spongy ground on some sort of cloth or blanket. Wrapped in it.

Low, deep voices rumbled nearby and when she finally gathered enough strength to open her eyes, the first thing she saw was a small orange glow. This was a fire, rather than the bowl of coals she remembered from…before. A little shiver caught her by surprise, followed by a whirlwind of vague images and sensations. Jane bit her lip as a twinge of lust pulsed sharply through her.

Two men sat near the small blaze, one on each side. They were talking, each holding a cup, one of them holding a curling piece of paper clear of the flames. They appeared to be examining it. Jane saw the silhouette of a bottle outlined by the fire. And the long, lean rod of a rifle, leaning against a nearby tree.

It was still night, and they were in the middle of the jungle…with no protection except for a bit of flame and a single weapon. Yet, the men appeared to be at ease, deep in discussion.

With effort, she dragged herself into a sitting position. Her hair cascaded down around her shoulders and torso, wildly curly and tangled, somehow freed from its knot. The blanket fell away and left her breasts and belly bare. As if puppet heads drawn by a string, both men turned to look at her.

Jane felt a rush of heat over her cheeks as she looked at Jonathan and then Kellan. In a flash, she remembered everything that happened. Everything she'd hoped and planned for when she left the treehouse that evening for a walk with her fiancé…and that which she hadn't expected. The heat on her face burned stronger with the memory of Kellan, groaning and straining against her. His hands caressing, fingers poking and stroking, as if he owned her.

"Jane," said Jonathan. He tucked the paper away and reached out a hand toward her. "Love, come join us. It's warm here." She could see he was dressed only in a pair of trousers.

She pulled slowly to her feet, gathering the blanket up with her. Her clothing must be nearby.

How should she act? How could she face Kellan again…or even Jonathan, after their actions in the pool? An unexpected shudder sizzled through her as she remembered the feel of that dark, tight orgasm, the way she'd felt uncomfortably full and strange during the experience.

She was confused and slow, her mind muddled, her muscles weak from the effects of the extreme heat and the cloying smoke, along with the intense physical experience. For a moment, she considered turning and running into the jungle, away from them. But this was Jonathan, her lost love. And he'd…shared her with Kellan. Shared her.

Jon, you gave your word.

You have my blessing.

Yes, Jonathan had given her to Kellan with his blessing. His *permission*. Why or how would he do such a thing? And how could she have enjoyed it?

Her cheeks flamed hotter. As strange and unsettling as it had been, she couldn't deny that she'd found pleasure beneath two sets of hands, pinioned between two bodies. So much pleasure that she could hardly walk, and wasn't even certain she had the energy to speak.

"Jane, come sit with me," her fiancé said. "You were so incredibly lovely tonight."

She wanted to talk to him about it, to rail at him…but she didn't want to do so in front of Kellan. His dark eyes followed her as she made her way to sit next to Jonathan, sinking to the ground next to him. The flare of lust was there, as it had always been. She shivered. But now he knew…now he'd tasted her.

Would he want more?

Did she? Her arsehole twinged at the thought. A tight, sharp reminder that she'd reached an orgasm unlike anything she'd experienced.

As if reading her mind, Kellan said, "You seem to have enjoyed losing your second maidenhead, Jane." His smile could only be described as a satisfied leer. "It was my pleasure to induct you into that particular form of eroticism."

"Now, Kel," Jonathan said, smoothing his hand roughly over the top of Jane's head and down over her long curls. "Don't mortify her. Jane is a proper lady."

"What did you mean, he promised you?" Jane finally found the words. She looked at Kellan, meeting his gaze with as much steadiness as she could muster. The fog was beginning to fade.

Kellan was taking a drink from his cup—a vessel she recognized as being from the treehouse. He'd been well-prepared when he came to join them. As he pulled the mug away, he smiled. "I made no secret of my attraction for you. Jon helped with that by telling me stories of your passion and how responsive you were."

"But Jonathan, why would you—"

Her fiancé smiled at her fondly. "What else were we to do on that long ocean voyage, all those days and nights of nothing to do? I love you and was proud of you and couldn't stop thinking of you, Jane. And these last three years, I dreamt of you every night. I missed you so."

Before she could respond, he pulled her face toward his, covering her mouth with full, demanding lips. He tasted of whiskey, strong and pungent. His hand slipped down to pull the blanket away, but Jane dragged it back up. She twisted her face from his and sat back, breathing heavily. "Jonathan, what are you doing?"

He gave a low chuckle. "Such fire you have, Jane, darling. It matches your hair. I love to see you riled." His eyes, she saw now, were glazed. He was very drunk.

"Jane." Kellan's voice drew her attention from Jonathan, and she turned. Their eyes met across the flames, and she saw at once that though Jonathan was in his cups, his friend was not only dressed, but fully sober. For some reason, this realization made her become even more alert.

"What did you mean about Jonathan promising you? What did he promise?" she asked.

"I promised him," Jonathan said, his words a little slurred, "if I ever saw you again...if he brought you to me...he could—"

"What do you mean, if you ever saw me again?" For the first time since waking, Jane sat up straight, at full attention.

"Jane, darling...as much as I appreciate the view," Kellan broke in, "you must take care with that blanket. It's nearly in the fire." His gaze dropped pointedly to her bare breasts. "If you're chilled, come sit next to me. I would be happy to warm you."

She yanked the blanket up again, trying to make sense of a conversation that stopped and started and followed detours. "What did he mean?" she demanded of Kellan. "How could he have known he wouldn't see me again? And why would he—"

Kellan was shaking his head. "No, no, Jane…he's not making sense. I know. He's had too much whiskey. Forgive him. He is still suffering from shock at finding you again. And it's been many years since he drank whiskey—I daresay he wasn't prepared for the result."

"Tell me why you said that," she insisted.

"It was a jest we both made when we first arrived here in Madagascar. A poorly-timed jest, frankly, in which he promised if he ever saw you again, he'd allow me to…well, Jane…knowing what I know about you, and your…passionate nature, I'm sure you wondered what it would be like with two men." His eyes were little more than dark spots in his shadowed face. "And you're too much of a proper lady to actually agree to such a thing…even though you clearly enjoyed it. Didn't you?"

She swallowed hard. How could it be? He was correct. She had enjoyed it…yet….

"It happened we made that joke the very night before Jonathan became lost," Kellan explained. "Poor timing, and yet…it all worked out well, did it not?" He reached out his hand for her. "I made no secret how I felt about you Jane. Surely you cannot hold it against me, that I desire you."

"But it wasn't Jonathan's permission to *give*," she told him, at last finding the strength to be angry. She ignored his hand. "It was mine."

Before Kellan could respond, a low growl rolled through the night. Jane gasped and turned to look into the shadows. Kellan jumped to his feet and snatched up his rifle as Jonathan staggered upright.

"Leopard," Kellan said, aiming his firearm into the darkness. The tall grass waved eerily in a non-existent breeze.

"An angry one from the sound," Jonathan said, dragging his shirt on with awkward movements. "I'll get a torch."

Jane pulled to her feet, heart pounding, staring into the

darkness. Would the beast come charging into the clearing? She edged away from the shadows, clinging to her blanket.

The growl came again, followed by a roar that sent a horrible shiver down her spine. "It's coming closer!" she cried just as Jonathan said, "It's angry! It must have a mate or den nearby—"

"Or a kill," Kellan said. His voice was grim and he aimed his rifle into the shadows. "I hope we aren't between it and whatever it's after."

Jane looked frantically around for her clothing and finally spied the white bundle. She wanted more than a simple blanket between her and an infuriated leopard. But before she could even pick up the chemise, there was a loud rustle. This time it came from a different direction. Behind her.

A chill ran down her spine. Was Kellan right? Were they caught between the cat and its mate or kits?

"Quick, Jane, climb up that tree," Jonathan said. His voice no long slurred, but was tight with alarm. He lifted a long, thick stick from the fire, flames blazing from it.

She stumbled toward the tree he indicated, all the while watching with wide eyes as the two men faced the shadows, back to back. Kellan's rifle seemed puny in comparison to the mental image she had of a leopard. Another growl rumbled through the dark, closer. She fancied she could see its eyes, glowing from the shadows. The sight raised the hair on the back of her neck and she scrabbled for the lowest branch of the tree.

It was barely possible to hold the blanket in place and attempt to climb, but Jane managed to do so. At least she'd have some protection against the rough bark or the sharp, fine twigs that might scratch her sensitive skin. She pulled herself up with great effort, climbing onto a nearby stump to help. She was crawling onto the second-lowest branch just as a massive cat streaked into the clearing in a long, low pounce. He was no more than a man's height below her.

She bit her lip, holding back a scream as Kellan fired. He either missed or the bullet was no deterrent, for the leopard—sleek in its spotted golden coat—gave no pause. It landed in front of the two men with a roar.

Jonathan swung the torch at the feline as Kellan dodged its great, clawed paw. The cat reared back, ready to strike. Jane, already climbing to the next branch, saw the way its fur rose along its spine. It was infuriated. She couldn't see its face, for she was too high. But she imagined glowing green eyes and pointed fangs.

She wanted to cry out *Be careful, Jonathan!*, but she knew better than to distract him. In fact...she suddenly took note of her environment. Was there something she could do to distract the cat? Even injure it?

She put her hand down on a nearby branch, leaning forward into the thick branches of the trees growing close to hers. *The branch moved.*

Jane screamed as the smooth, dry scales of a snake registered in her mind. She jolted back and away, nearly losing her balance in the tree, and then...before she could think too hard about it, she jabbed at the thick body of the snake with another branch. It stiffened and hissed, as thick as her wrist, coiling itself together. But the head was in the opposite direction and she must have taken it by surprise, perhaps waking it. Jane gave a good, sharp jab at the head with the forked stick to hold it off, then used her hand to yank the creature off the branch. She flung it away and watched it fall, tumbling in a tangled mass to the ground.

Bile rose in her throat as she realized what she'd done: she'd *touched a snake*. She'd not only touched a snake, but she'd poked at it, lifted it, pulled it, thrown it to the ground....

Whether it was a poisonous snake or otherwise dangerous, she didn't want to know. She simply tried to keep from vomiting (it could have bitten her!) and looked down. She saw that the snake landed in the middle of the clearing, in front of the leopard.

And the snake was furious.

It rose in front of the cat and, as Jane watched, Jonathan and Kellan tried to circle around from behind. The leopard and snake seemed intent upon each other, and the two men began to ease away toward the edge of the clearing. They could disappear into the darkness and they would be safe.

Jane was about to call out to them to go, when the tree in which she was perched gave the faintest shiver. And then all at once *he* was there.

The wild man.

She would have gasped, or even screamed, if she hadn't been so startled. If it hadn't been so sudden, his appearance… as if from thin air. As it was, she merely stopped breathing for a moment.

He crouched on an adjacent branch, his eyes meeting hers in the moonlight. They were close enough that she smelled the cinnamon essence on his breath and the fresh, jungle scent that always accompanied him. His broad, muscular shoulders were glazed with silvery light, and one hand rose, grasping a thick liana vine above his head. The bulge of muscle in his flexed arm was outlined and Jane found herself breathing again. Rapidly. Heat rushed through her.

Before she could react, he reached for her, curling an arm around her waist, lifting her toward him. And the next thing she knew, they were airborne, swinging past branches, through leaves…and *up*.

Jane gasped as he landed surefooted on a wide branch much higher off the ground than her perch. By now, she was clinging to him, her arms around his neck, his warm, firm torso pressed against hers….

And she realized with a shock that somewhere along the

way, the blanket had slipped from her grasp. She was naked, her breasts wedged against his chest, her bare legs straddling his cloth-covered waist. The graze of the hair on his thighs brushed against her sensitive skin, and she had to lift her face to keep from burying it in a warm, male-scented shoulder.

Then she forgot her immodesty, for they were gliding through the air once more. So smoothly and rapidly, it was as if they were flying. And not like the hot air balloons back home that merely floated wherever the wind took them, but with speed and dexterity. Her loose hair ruffled, fluttering and tangling behind them. His muscles bunched and stretched, sleek and firm, and as they swung from vine to vine, the leaves brushed over her like a gentle breeze.

How did he know where to reach in this darkness? How did he so unerringly find the next vine in the shadows? The thought made her tense for a moment and close her eyes, as if to ward off the possibility that they might suddenly tumble to the ground.

Then Jane relaxed. He showed no hesitation in his movements. He obviously had been traveling like this for a long time. He was as skilled as the sweet little chimps she'd seen at the circus, and had yet to see here.

But this man was no sweet little chimp.

As she clung to him, Jane couldn't banish the memory of the night he visited her in her treehouse bedchamber. His hands were gentle, almost reverent. His eyes covered her, drinking in the sight of her as if she were some great object of beauty. But his mouth...his gentle, exploratory, sleek mouth, buried between her legs....

Jane's mouth went dry as she remembered him, lifting his face from her wet, swollen quim, and meeting her eyes in the low light. His lips were full and glistened from her juices, and his firm hand still curled darkly against her thigh. She invited him to her, beckoning him close...and then he heard the snake rustling across the floor.

Whatever might have happened between them was interrupted as the wild man battled the snake, writhing on the floor with the massive reptile. Jane retrieved her pistol and got close enough to shoot it in the head while he held it still. Then he disappeared through the window when everyone else came to investigate the ruckus, and Jane was left satisfied—oh, indeed—and yet wanting more.

She couldn't contain a small shiver of anticipation. What would happen now?

Where was he taking her?

Her question was soon answered when they landed on the massive branch of a wide-reaching tree. To her surprise, the spread of branches held a treehouse, smaller and less complicated than her own.

He held onto her until her feet were stable and then released her gently and gestured toward the structure. "Go," he said in his deep voice. Jane did as he bid, taking a mere two steps along the branch to the entrance.

She didn't have to duck in order to get through opening, and inside she was struck by the neatness of the place, its compact size, and the fact that its walls and roof weren't in the best of condition. Either this treehouse had been built many years before the one she and her companions inhabited, or it hadn't been as well-maintained. Regardless, it was obviously a home built in European style (as much as one could take into account in the jungle)—not at all like something the natives might have built, if one believed Con Bellingworth's *Pictorial of the Madagascan Jungle.*

Of course, Bellingworth also claimed there were no leopards or dangerous wild cats anywhere in Madagascar...but he was obviously wrong.

Jane stepped in and then hesitated. What if another snake—or something worse—was inside? It was too dark to see much, and she'd had her fill of slithering reptiles in the last two days.

The wild man seemed to understand her hesitation, for he eased past her into the small space. After a brief moment of listening to him rustle about, she heard a soft, sharp scraping noise. He was crouched in the corner of the small treehouse, his arms moving back and forth rapidly over something on the floor. She inched closer and saw that he was rubbing a slender stick quickly and forcefully back and forth along the narrow groove in a small, stripped log. After only a few moments, she smelled smoke and then light flared in the tinder that had been shaved from the log.

He bent over the young flame and blew long and gently. The tiny fire shifted and expanded, billowing into a small blaze. When he looked up at her, his face limned by the golden glow, Jane's heart stopped.

He was breathtaking.

Their eyes met and once again she became conscious of her nakedness. But it wasn't shame that brought a warmth to her cheeks.

He held out a hand to her and Jane, her heart thudding like a drum, stepped toward him.

Now that there was illumination, she could see more of the treehouse's interior. There was a bed, large enough for two people. It appeared to be well-kept, and even the coverings on it seemed clean and inviting. No pillow. Three large steamer trunks sat to one side. A crude desk was built into the wall, with a massive stump for a chair. And she noticed in the corner a small box on tall legs, filled with soft cloth. And a small stuffed bear. Her heart swelled. A baby's crib.

At once a myriad of thoughts rushed through her; perhaps a good distraction from the fact that she was naked and alone with the wild man once again. She looked at him, wondering. His blue eyes and relatively light skin clearly indicated he was European, or perhaps even American. Did this dwelling belong to him or his family? Had he been shipwrecked, like Robinson Crusoe, but with a wife and child? Could he have been the child who slept in that crib and somehow been separated from his parents? Raised by the wolves like the storybook character Mowgli?

Or was it possible he had simply found this place accidentally? Did he even live here?

His hand solid and firm around her fingers, the wild man brought her to the bed and, heart still racing, Jane perched on the edge of it. She took no notice of her nudity any longer. She saw that he'd contained the fire in a small metal tinderbox, obviously left by the previous occupants of this place.

She looked up at him, their eyes meeting in the dancing light. The desire she saw there made her breath catch. Despite her earlier activity, a sharp dart of lust stabbed her, and she moistened her lips with her tongue. The wild man's eyes fell to her mouth and seemed to catch there for the longest moment.

Jane still couldn't breathe. She couldn't imagine wanting anything more at that moment than for him to bend to her and cover her mouth with his.

How can I think this way? I just left my fiancé, only moments ago.

The fiancé who'd promised her to, and shared her with, another man.

Jane firmed her lips and thrust the thoughts of Jonathan away, reaching to touch the wild man's chest. It was just in front of her, slightly above eye-level. She hardly had to stretch out her arm. Her fingers settled against the firm planes of his torso, in the shallow indentation between two flat slabs of breast. The pounding of his heart thudded frantically beneath her fingers. His skin was warm, the color of shelled almonds in the daylight, but tonight it was a rich caramel hue in the glow of fire. A light smattering of hair grew there, turning darker and thicker in a line that traveled below his navel. He wore a cloth around his waist made of animal skin.

She felt his breathing stop, his body still and become so taut it seemed to quiver.

Then, before she could reach for him, he stepped back. Her hand fell to her lap and she looked up at him, confused and questioning.

He gestured to the bed, and, drawing one of the coverings up and away, indicated that she was to lie down.

Bewildered and yet touched, Jane did so. The platform was covered with a large silky fur and despite her expectation, it wasn't hot or heavy. Instead, the skin was soft and inviting.

No sooner had she reclined than he settled the blanket over her in a waft of sweet, light cloth. She had a brief moment to wonder where he'd obtained such a thing. Whatever filled the mattress was both soft and firm, and Jane suddenly realized how exhausted she was. Exhausted, sore…and overwhelmed.

She looked up at the wild man and smiled. How had he known?

But…. She lifted herself up on one elbow, holding the blanket modestly to her chest. "Woman," she said, touching herself between the breasts. Then she gestured toward him, brushing his torso once again with her fingers as he crouched next to her. "Man."

He nodded. His heart thudded hard beneath her touch. "Man." He covered her hand with his strong, callused fingers, then moved it back to her chest. Heavy and warm. "Woman."

She nodded, then, when he would have taken his hand away, she shifted and held it firmly in her fingers, still at her breast. "Jane," she told him, flattening his hand against her. "Jane."

His eyes lit with comprehension. "Szzzzhaaaayn. Szhane," he repeated. His voice was reverent. "Jane. Woman."

"Jane," she said once more. Then she moved their clasped hands to touch him again and waited, still propped on her elbow.

He understood immediately. "Zaren. Man." He thumped himself on the chest, losing his grip on her fingers in the process.

Jane smiled at him and eased back down on the bed. At last. The wild man had a name. "Zaren," she whispered. "It suits you."

And she closed her eyes.

ZAREN WATCHED the woman for a long time.

Jane. She was called Jane. He smiled, something inside him expanding into a great warmth. *Jane.*

He settled the small fire, safely contained in a metal box, on the stump and admired how the light and shadow danced over her lovely face. Beauty that made his insides hurt.

He wanted to touch her fire-hair, now glowing even brighter in the light of the dancing flames. The coils of it spilled in luminous tangles over her ivory shoulder and onto the sleeping place. But he didn't wish to disturb her. He could watch over her, and she would sleep in peace.

If she slept, she trusted him.

The scent of her—the musky, sweet, special essence—filled his nostrils and would permeate the place she slept. He would have that memory of her after she was gone from here. Her fingers relaxed, curled under her cheek. Her breathing changed, slowing and deepening. Her lips, crushed against her hand, eased into the shape of a soft, tempting flower bud.

He wanted to press his mouth to hers. He had tasted her before, there, in that sweet, warm, slick place between her legs…but now he knew he wanted to touch her lips. And all the other parts of her.

Beneath the antelope skin he wore around his waist, Zaren's

rod shifted and swelled at the idea. He frowned down at it and turned his thoughts elsewhere. He had no patience, no time for that now.

He had much to think about. He wasn't certain he understood what happened this day.

It seemed that the light-skinned man, the one who was new to the area, belonged to Jane.

Zaren saw, watching from his usual high perch among the thick leaves. He understood the language of bodies in all types of animals, and when Jane and the new man came together in an embrace, he recognized that they knew each other. They belonged together. She was overjoyed to see him, clinging to his arm as if she would never let him leave.

The other man, the one who had tried to mate with Jane when she didn't want to, watched from a distance. His expression was empty, but the way he stood was not. Zaren thought he knew how he felt.

Zaren went away after that, swinging too fast and too hard through the trees. He misjudged once and fell the distance of a python before grabbing a solid enough vine to stop his tumble. He hadn't made a mistake like that since he was a young cub, showing off for his wolf siblings. But something inside his chest hurt, burned, and he was angry enough at himself, at the woman and her mate, to hurtle off a high branch into the cold, deep river instead of wading in.

He emerged from the icy water with nothing but a scraped knee and bruised shoulder, then narrowly missed being attacked by a crocodile. Its jaws snapped closed behind his heel just as Zaren yanked himself up and out of the water using a low branch. Foolish. Foolish and blind as a snake, he'd been.

It was then he knew he mustn't blame the woman. He wasn't angry with her. She belonged with the new man. He was her mate, and mates stayed together until one of them died. Just as the wolves who raised him had done.

Still, Zaren had been curious, and later that night, unable to sleep in his cool, dark cave, he emerged. He meant to look on her one more time. And to see if the mate slept with her. He wondered how he would feel, seeing the mate's body curved around the soft, curvy, sweet-scented skin he'd come to crave.

The image rose in his mind and it made Zaren both hot and chilled.

But when he reached her nest—the same place he battled a rock snake last night—it was empty. Perched in the window, he sniffed the air, but the new man's scent was not mingled with Jane's. He had not been in the nest.

It was simple for Zaren to find her after that. But when he looked down at the clearing with the hot, bubbling pool of water, she was sleeping on the ground. Her mate was with the other light-skinned man, the non-mate. And they were talking, looking at a paper.

The scents on the air told him what had happened: mating. But he was confused by the three strong scents, and that of the lystra plant mingled with it all. How could three mate together? It wasn't possible. That wasn't how it was done. Only one male and one female.

He watched for a time, trying to understand, watching the men and watching…Jane. She rose and joined them at the fire, sitting near her mate. But there was something wrong about the men and the scene below.

He sniffed, listened, watched…but he couldn't understand what bothered him.

And then moments later, the leopard made her appearance, and Zaren took the opportunity to help the woman…Jane…escape. He realized he felt no compulsion to return and ensure the mate and non-mate were safe. They had fire, and one of them had the loud stick. They could evade the leopard if they were careful and smart.

He cared only for Jane's safety.

Now, he settled on the floor next to the…bed…yes, that was the word. He listened, sniffed, and looked around the small place. With the light flickering soft yellow and orange, sending gentle shadows dancing, it was warm and cozy and safe. He remembered…something…something like this….

But his head hurt. The sharp pain chased the hovering memory away and instead, he closed his eyes. He could rest as well.

The slightest sound, the barest shift in the wind, even the most gentle waft of a change of scent, would awaken him. She was safe, and he, for the first time, slept, breathing the comfort and pleasure of her essence.

VI

WHEN JANE OPENED HER EYES, it was to daylight... and a very intense blue gaze looking down at her.

"Zaren," she said, and reached for his hand when he would have moved it away.

"Jane," he whispered, and left his fingers on the edge of the bed, covered by hers.

She looked down, lifting his hand to examine it. Tanned deep brown, rough, sprinkled with hair on the back. Wide, callused, the underside broad and tough and slightly more pale. His nails clean and short, one of them black from an injury. Scratches, some new, some healed. His fingers...long and elegant. One of them had been up inside her. She shivered.

Jane looked back up at him and their eyes met again. Heat raged between them and her insides fluttered and seemed to take flight. He seemed to be drinking in the sight of her as he did every time they were together. She wished she knew what he was thinking. She wished she could speak with him.

She might have reached for him. She almost did, pulling him to her...but then he moved away, like a skittish cat. How could such a strong, powerful man be so uncertain?

But when he looked at her, the expression in his eyes wasn't uncertain. It was enough to make her melt into a puddle of hot lantern oil.

And why was she thinking about him that way? She had a fiancé. Jonathan. Whom she loved. She truly, truly loved.

Zaren had turned away, and now he offered her a small cup and two small bowls carved from wood. Water? No. She sniffed the contents of the cup. Tea? She frowned and sniffed again. The liquid was warm, and it had a scent to it. Some sort of jungle tea. Had he heated the water with his small fire, or had he found natural water from the hot springs? She wished she knew how to ask; she was becoming more curious about this man every moment.

She sipped the tea and tasted cinnamon and other fresh, astringent flavors. It made her mouth feel clean and alive. The other two bowls contained berries and nuts. Jane realized she was hungry. She glanced at him.

Shy *and* thoughtful.

To her relief, he didn't watch her eat. She feared he would sit and gaze at her like she was an animal in a zoo. Instead, he drank from another cup, tossed a handful of berries into his own mouth, then turned and walked across the small room.

Jane watched him, realizing she'd never seen him actually walk. And he didn't precisely walk. He…strode. No, he…stalked. Prowled. Like a cat. With smooth and precise movements, covering the small space in four masterful strides.

He had long hair that reached past his shoulder blades, and it was in a style she'd never seen before encountering him. Long, soft coils. Springy to the touch, about the width of a finger. His body, though very muscular, was nevertheless lean. And although he was covered from the waist down, she had a view of his broad shoulders and the sleek muscles of his back.

When he turned, she realized he'd been digging in one of the trunks she'd noticed last night. And now he held a…*book*. He looked at her, and the expression in his face nearly broke her heart.

It was a combination of apprehension and hope. Fear and

determination. Question and trust. His eyes were so blue.

Jane sat up, holding the blanket modestly over her breasts. "What is it?" she asked, uncertain what caused such a range of emotion. "Is that yours?"

He brought the book and sat next to her on the bed. His warm skin brushed against her arm and Jane had to draw in a steadying breath when his touch seemed to sear into her, leaving a residual mark.

The book was old, filled with large images and simple words. A child's pictorial dictionary. Jane noticed his knuckles were white as he held the book open in his lap, and felt intensity quivering from his very being. Apprehension? Hope? What was it?

He pointed to the drawing of a woman. "Woman," he said, his voice low and rumbly. Then he pointed to a man. "Man," he said with more confidence.

Jane nodded next to him; they had already established his mastery of those words. Man. Woman.

Zaren. Jane.

Man fuck woman. The phrase popped into her head suddenly and she almost gasped at her mind's inappropriate waywardness. *Zaren fuck Jane.* Oh, *yesss*....She closed her eyes for a moment to control her heightened breathing.

She didn't think the word *fuck* would appear in the child's book. But she was certain it wouldn't be difficult to communicate that, at least.

He pointed to another picture, then looked at her. "Woof." There was question in his blue eyes now.

The word under the picture said *dog*. Jane pointed to the drawing and said, "Dog." Then she made a barking sound, like a *woof.* Zaren looked at her, quizzically, then, humor in his eyes, he barked back at her.

His sounded much more authentic. So much so that she looked around to make certain there wasn't a real dog in the vicinity.

Then, his sensual lips still quirked with humor, he looked back down at the book. "Dawg. Dog. Woof?" Then he turned quickly through the pages of the book, which had clearly been thumbed through many times. She caught flashes of birds, beetles and butterflies, apples, bananas, beds, elephants, tigers, and…a wolf.

Zaren pointed at the picture of a wolf. "Woof. Dog."

Now she understood. The pictures were similar and yet different. She pointed to the trees growing around the wolf, the impression of a rugged environment. Then she traced a finger around the animal itself. "Wolf." She turned the pages of the book back to the picture of the dog, which stood next to a family. "Dog." She gestured to the father, mother and child next to their pet.

Zaren frowned at the pictures for a long while, flipping back and forth, murmuring the two different words. Then at last he looked at her, comprehension shining in his blue eyes. He made a gruntlike sound that sounded like an affirmative.

She smiled at him, and for a moment, she thought she might simply tumble into his gaze and stay there forever. Her pulse pounded in her throat, surely audible to him. Then, as if by some instinct, they both turned back to the book. She began to point out more words for him, drawing imaginary lines between the figures to indicate their relationship.

"Man. Father. Woman. Mother. Boy. Son."

He repeated all of the words, clearly becoming more confident as they went on. It became easier for him to speak the word correctly the first time, and on the very last picture, he actually said it with her.

"Fam-ly."

Jane looked at him in surprise as shock registered on his own face. Then he smiled with delight, a great, wide beaming grin that crinkled the corners of his eyes and made a gentle crease along one side of his lips. His eyes danced with triumph and Jane's mouth went dry. *This man....*

She had the overwhelming urge to reach for him, to curl her fingers around that solid warm arm brushing against hers and pull him to her. Pleasure and lust shot in a hot rush down between her legs, and she suddenly felt hot and prickly and *aware.*

Zaren stilled for a moment, his slender nostrils lifting, then flaring slightly as if catching a scent on the air. His fingers tightened over the book, shifting it almost imperceptibly, and she felt the muscles in his arm tighten next to hers.

She was close enough to see the hard pulse pounding in his golden throat, and the faint sheen over his skin. Something warm and male filled the air, the scent of him. Her nipples tightened and heat flushed over her chest, spreading down to where she was already swelling and dampening.

He held the book in his lap, and Jane reached for it, clumsily. He jolted when she brushed against the rigid cock that rose beneath the book and his loincloth. His mouth tightened, outlined with white tension, and he stared down at the book that now rested more on her lap than his. He even pointed to the drawing of a cat.

"Cat," she said. Puss. *Pussy.* She swallowed hard. *Someone's pussy is getting wet.* Her face was hot. Her breathing unsteady. Her nipples tight and ready.

"Cat," he repeated, somehow ignoring the upright pitch in the center of his loincloth.

Jane wasn't looking at the pictures any longer. She pulled the book from his hands and set it on the floor. And then, giving herself no chance to reconsider, she knelt in front of him, between his legs.

Zaren's eyes went round with shock, and then dark as his irises sprang wide and black. His body stilled; she'd never felt anyone become so instantly still. He didn't breathe. She swore even his pulse stopped as she pulled the soft hide away from him. Not a hair quivered, not an eyelash flickered as he looked down at her hands as they settled at the juncture of his thighs, bracketing his turgid cock and tight, hot sac.

Jane's mouth watered, and her quim was full and wet to match. She pressed her knees together and felt tiny throbbing pulses of the little pearl in her damp heat. They shuddered up through her body.

He was magnificent. Everything a man like him should be: thick and hard, a beautiful, ready purple-red, smooth and bulging with veins. Fairly quivering with attention. A shiny drop hung from the tip and Jane leaned forward to swipe it away with a quick, light flick.

When her tongue touched the salty drop, Zaren gave a low, tortured gasp, and all at once he was alive again. Moving, breathing, his pulse raging through his veins, his skin shivering and his muscles quivering…all of this beneath her hands, against her arms propped on his bent thighs. She heard his expulsion of breath in relief and pleasure and felt a sharp ripple go through him.

She looked up at him now. His eyes were shining, dark orbs fiercely focused on her…no, on his cock. Still framed by her hands, still proud and turgid and trembling. His cheeks were flushed, his lips parted.

And then she noticed his fingers. Curled into the edge of the bed, taut and white and rigid, so tight they trembled. The tendons in his hands and arms stood out in sharp relief.

Emboldened and filled with lust, Jane smoothed her hands closer together, cupping his quivering cock. He was hot and hard, and she grasped him, able to fit her fingers around his girth with only a little overlap. Heat surged through her as she imagined the sensation of this massive rod filling her. Her tiny pearl gave an urgent little pulse, remembering his busy, sleek tongue teasing it. She slid her other hand under the tight, warm sac and lightly brushed her fingers through the hair springing from it.

All of her attention was on the magnificent tool in her hands, and she stroked him once, then a second time, her hand moving long and slow along the velvety length, enjoying the heat and vibration, the length and the texture. She felt him surge beneath her fingers, the veins swelling and filling, semen hurtling up toward the head, filling his cock, ready to shoot free. His thighs vibrated against her torso. Then, fairly drooling with anticipation, she swallowed back her desire and curved both hands around his cock and closed tightly. Fisted hard around him, she made him gasp and still once more. Then, with one more tight, sharp stroke from base to head, she brought him up and over. He cried out as his rod exploded, spurting over her arms and onto her bare chest.

He pulsed and surged in her hand, his body relaxing back onto his elbows, his desperate grip loosening from the bed. His eyes were closed, his head sagged back, exposing his long, strong throat. His pulse pounded there, his warm skin glistened, his chest heaved, thick coils of hair clung to his skin. Beautiful. Edible. Jane moaned.

And then all at once, he moved. One moment, he was collapsed, sated, on the bed…the next, he was *there.* Jane hardly had a moment to catch her breath, to recognize the change in him before she was flung onto the bed, whipped up and onto her back with a sudden whoosh. He was *there*, hard and strong and powerful, over her. His hands covered her body, cupping her jaw, sliding down over her shoulders to fill themselves with her breasts. His mouth tasted, licked, nibbled, hot and rough and ravenous. His weight was heavy, solid, pinning her to the bed, his legs twined with hers.

He was everywhere, powerful and dangerous, the animal unleashed. Even the sounds he made…low, primal growls and rumbles he made from deep in his chest…were wild. Primitive.

And they touched her, titillated her. The simple, feral timbre vibrated in her ear, shivering in delicious, deep licks down her spine as she realized how untamed this man was.

And that she had set him free.

For a moment, fear mingled with wild, hot pleasure as she imagined him impaling her with his massive self, slamming into her, filling her, riding her. She groaned in desperation and desire. *Yes. Please.* Her quim pulsed with need, swollen and dripping. *Zaren...fuck...Jane.*

Hot and strong, he bent over her, forcing her in place as his mouth sucked on a nipple, drawing it deep into his mouth while she writhed beneath him, arching up, twisting, for *more*. The sharp sensation jolted through her, pleasure hot and sharp jagged down to her belly, tightening her quim painfully. She cried out in desperation, shifting her hips, curling her legs around his waist, trying to bring him back down to her. Down there. *There*, where the fire raged.

He was hot against her, burning into her skin, rough with hair and firm with sleek, damp muscle. His hands grasped and stroked, shifted her roughly, as if she were his prey, as if he owned her. He ate at her, sucking her nipple so hard she suddenly exploded into a shocking orgasm that wrung through her limbs, leaving her weak and spent.

And then, with a barely audible growl, so deep and low it made every hair on her body rise, he turned to her other breast. Still, there was no adoration here, no tenderness or uncertainty. He devoured, his tongue surging around the sensitive point, flickering and licking, swirling, and then he sucked and sucked, and she cried out, arching against him, knowing if he drew her deeper, too deep, she would explode. He teased—how did he know how to *tease*?—flickering over the very most sensitive tip of her tight, rosy, swollen nipple.

Jane felt warm skin shifting, powerful and taut, beneath her hands. She clawed and begged, but he was relentless, determined, wild. He held her firmly, pinned her down, torturing her with his rough lips, his punishing mouth leaving her taut, wet nipple bare and throbbing. She hurt, she ached, she burned and then something touched her between her legs…the barest pressure, the lightest touch, sliding through her wetness. Jane gave a desperate little scream and the pressure moved away before she could snatch in another breath and beg more.

She arched up, twisted desperately, her vision flushed red with desire, her body hot and damp everywhere, her long hair plastered to her, tangling around them, her legs wrapped around his. "Please…please," she managed to gasp, her nails tearing into his skin. "*Zaren.*"

He made a sound, wild and low, and suddenly she was airborne. The bed slammed into her face and shoulders, her knees were yanked apart as she pulled herself up on her arms. Strong hands gripped her hips and Jane whimpered with relief as she spread her legs farther.

She waited, quivering, trembling, throbbing, her thighs wide, her swollen labia full and open, ready and dripping. She heard a low sound, almost like a sigh, but more like a growl or an animal's groan, and then he was there. Hard and hot, thick and long. She released a relieved gasp, very nearly cried, when he shoved inside her.

They both moaned, both sounds of pleasure mixed with the pain of waiting. His fingers tight at her hips, holding her as if he were afraid she was going to bolt, he didn't wait. One moment he was sliding into her sheath, and the next, he was slamming into her, thrusting wildly and forcefully as she gripped the bed, slamming back into him, meeting him with her own strokes. *Yes, yes, yes….*

He arched over her, dominant, wild, slamming into her from behind with primal pleasure, powerful and strong. He was unleashed, primitive, a wild being forcibly mating with his partner. Taking. Driven by need and instinct.

The intensity was too much. She was overcome by hot rolling pleasure, sharp, hard stabbing desire…swelling, surging…and then her world shattered into starry release, warm, sweet, liquid relief. Tears gathered and fell, and, her mouth open in a silent cry of jubilation and pleasure, Jane collapsed onto her face as he swelled, pulsed, and slammed against her once more.

His groan of triumph and satiation filled her ears, prickling over her skin, then settled on her like a hot, damp blanket. His cock pulsed inside her, still thick and full, and then she felt his fingers relax. He held himself upright for a moment longer, then fell away as if utterly spent, collapsing next to her.

Jane's wobbly knees and trembling arms gave out and she tumbled down next to him, her body still trembling and throbbing its gentle gratitude.

Warm, damp skin meshed together. She closed her eyes, her lips curved in a private smile. Her body still shuddered gently, as if clinging to the last licks of pleasure, then eased. All was quiet.

All was good.

JANE DREAMT VAGUE DREAMS.

She was swimming. She was rocking and swaying and gliding. She was bundled close and she sensed the warm breeze sliding over her, gentle and comforting. She felt warm arms around her, strong and sure, and she was weightless, floating on a sea of pleasure and satiation.

"Jane."

Someone was calling her from far away. She nestled back into the warmth of Zaren's arms. Smelled his delicious scent. Remembered the wild urges—

"Jane! Oh, my stars, *Jane!*"

The shrill voice, very nearby, had her eyes springing open.

Her environment was so disconnected from her dreams, from her memories and expectations, that it took her a long moment to comprehend.

Efremina stood, staring down at her, shocked and wide-eyed. "You're here! She's *here!* She's been here all along!" Her booming voice, filled with relief and shock of her own, filled the air in a great bellow, causing Jane to want to cover her ears and huddle…somewhere.

But there was nowhere to huddle, except here, in her very own bed. In her treehouse chamber bedroom.

She was home. Had she never left? Had it all been a dream?

Blinking, looking around, she tried to put the pieces together. They were jagged memories, none of them quite clear. None of them logical, either. She shook her head and realized it was tender and achy.

And when she tried to sit up, she realized two things simultaneously: she was nude under the blankets...and she was sore. Everywhere.

Everywhere.

All at once, before she was able to determine what happened, her father's bald head appeared at the doorway. "Janie!" he exclaimed. "Thank the stars you're safe!"

"We never thought to look here for you," Efremina was saying. "When Mr. Darkdale and Mr. Jonathan came back, they said you were missing. We didn't know where you'd been. She's back! She's here!" she screeched, cupping her hands around her mouth and directing her voice out the large window.

The window. Where the wild man...Zaren...had perched only nights ago.

"Why on earth would we think to look for you here?" Efremina said, as if still trying to convince herself. "Why, we wouldn't, would we?" she demanded of Jane's father. "She left with Mr. Jonathan, and he came back without her. He's been terribly worried," she said, now focusing on Jane. "He said how you was stalked by a leopard, and got separated when you tried to escape."

Jane's thoughts were finally coalescing. Yes. She'd gone for a walk with Jonathan...there was the interlude in the bubbling pool, all hot and wet and lust-fogged. And Kellan Darkdale. An odd tremor shuddered through her—not wholly unpleasant. She pushed the memory away.

The leopard...that part she remembered, throwing the snake down to the ground...and then the wild man. There. With her.

And then.... Her face blossomed with heat and her insides

shivered wonderfully. She remembered him. Oh, yes, she remembered him. She closed her eyes and *remembered.*

"Jane!"

All at once, Jonathan was there, bursting into her treehouse chamber. "Thank Providence you're safe! Where did you go? How did you get back here? No one saw you. We found your blanket hanging from a tree branch…. I thought I'd lost you again, darling." He sat on the bed next to her.

At first, Jane couldn't look at him. She had so many conflicting feelings and she wasn't certain what he would see if he looked into her eyes.

She loved him. She wanted and desired him. And last night's events in the hot springs had been…adventurous. Surprising. Even pleasurable. Yet dark and unsettling.

Jonathan had made a mistake, allowing Kellan to join them in their sex play. She would make certain he never did such a thing again.

But what had happened later…in the small treehouse with the wild man…. Even as her mouth watered and pangs of lust licked at her insides, Jane realized she must put it away.

She had to forget about everything. Especially Zaren.

Such a thing could never happen again. She was betrothed to a man, a well-respected Englishman. She couldn't continue to have this sort of…*affaire*…with this wild jungle man who sneaked into her chamber, and glided with her through the air as if she were naught but a rag doll…who sneaked her back *into* her chamber with no one the wiser after fucking her senseless. Her lips eased into a smile.

Clever. Strong. Shy. Delicious.

"Jane?"

She blinked and looked at Jonathan again. His hazel eyes were filled with concern and relief. "I don't know how you got back here safely, but I am so relieved. Please…let's not ever be separated again."

"Of course not, Jonathan," she told him, and squeezed his hand. "I was sorry to cause you worry." She noticed Efremina give her father a pointed look, and gesture sharply to the door.

Jonathan's eyes narrowed in thought, and a little smirk quirked his lips. "Dare I ask how you are feeling today? After… last night." His voice dropped low and deep, reminding her suddenly and starkly of the expression on his face when she was poised over him, being penetrated in the arse by his friend: bald lust, intense pleasure, possessiveness.

"I am a little…sore," she told him, glancing at the door as it closed behind Effie and Papa. "It was…unexpected, Jonathan. And I don't ever want—"

He was already shaking his head, his expression sober. "I know. I should never…well, you don't understand how he is," he said, his voice dropping low. "Darkdale can be very… persuasive, and he's not quite a gentleman about it. But it was no excuse for my…weakness. Jane, can you ever forgive me?"

It was as if a weight was lifted from her heart. "Yes, Jonathan. We all make mistakes." She couldn't help but think of herself, kneeling in front of Zaren…cupping his thick, ready cock, bending to lick its tip. She cleared her throat and pushed the image away. *No. Never again.* "Perhaps we can begin anew, now that I've found you once more? Put past mistakes behind us?"

"Thank you, Jane," he said, clasping her fingers tightly. "I thought I might have lost you in more ways than one. Now," he said, his grin turning even more mischievous. "I know the most perfect way to ease…*ahem*…soreness."

She smiled back. "And what is that, pray tell?"

"Sitting in a very warm, hot pool."

By daylight, being in the hot springs pool was a completely different experience than the dark, unsettling adventure of the night before. Jonathan sat on a rock as she stripped off her light cotton dress and laced-up chemise.

Jane slid gratefully into the steamy water, stifling a groan of pleasure. Despite the humidity and blazing sun, she welcomed the comfort of the hot springs.

As she relaxed in the water, feeling the soothing heat against her sore muscles and nether parts, Jane looked around. In the bright sunshine, she could see a riot of flowers in fuchsia, sapphire, fiery orange, and crimson. Leaves of all shades of green, aqua, and gray danced in the dappled light in a stunning variety of textures: furry, fuzzy, jagged, smooth, bumpy, ridged....

A small spotted lizard sunned himself on a rock, and a pair of bright purple and orange birds flew about in a sassy mating dance, flitting from tree to tree,and swooping low over Jane's head.

The jungle was filled with sound: the rustle of wind through the leaves, the songs of birds, the low calls of other land-bound animals, the rattling of branches and trunks as they clashed, the hiss from the water roiling around her.

Jane couldn't remember a time she'd been so silent, so aware of her environment. Certainly, she'd thought of the jungle as beautiful and wild—and dangerous!—but somehow, since arriving, she'd hardly taken the time to notice the details. She rested her head back against a stone, feeling perspiration gather on her nose and temples, allowing her arms and toes to float freely in the churning water.

Her breasts bobbed and swayed, her rosy nipples peeking out and then submerging as a wave licked over them. She glanced over to see if Jonathan had noticed, for he had promised to stand guard for snakes, leopards, and beady-eyed rodents.

He was gone. Jane frowned, but she wasn't concerned. He couldn't have gone far; he'd be within shouting distance. Perhaps he decided to give her a moment of privacy. Or perhaps *he'd* needed a moment of privacy.

She sank into the water and soaked her hair, her groan of pleasure mingling with the grumbling pool underwater. When she came up, Jonathan was still out of sight. Still unconcerned, she used the small pot of scented bicarbonate soda to wash her long, tangled hair and the rest of her body, then sunk back under again.

When she emerged and shook out the water from her ears, she realized that the jungle had gone silent. Eerily silent.

Jane sat up and looked around, suddenly tense. The small clearing was empty. Jonathan was gone, but her clothing was still laying over a small bush to air out.

"Jonathan?" she called, gathering up her hair into a bundle. She braided it quickly, in a thick plait, still looking around nervously.

There was a rustling the bushes, and Jonathan appeared.

"Oh, thank heavens," she said…and then she saw the angry-looking men behind him, dressed in native clothing and holding spears.

"Jane," said her lover in a tense voice. He held his arms away from his body as the natives prodded him forward by gesturing with their spears. "Stand up very slowly and carefully."

"Jonathan," she whispered, her eyes darting from him to the group of six men surrounding him. Two of them brandished spears at his chest.

The strangers looked ferocious and wild, with their faces painted in blue, white, yellow and green. Each had a red stripe bisecting his face. They wore loincloths just as Zaren had, but theirs were longer and fringed. Over each chest crossed two woven straps decorated with shells, feathers and…Jane swallowed…teeth. Aside from their clothing (or lack thereof), she recognized they must be from a native tribe by the dark hair and mahogany skin.

"What do they want?" she asked. "Do you know them? Are they the tribe you lived with?"

"Jane," Jonathan said again. "Stand up and come out of the pool slowly and carefully, or I'm afraid they might take out their impatience on me."

She bit her lip, still safely submerged in the water. Then, gathering her wits, she did as Jonathan bid and stood slowly. As the water sluiced off her, leaving her bare and wet, she felt each pair of eyes focus on her avidly. Her thick plait was of no help in providing modesty, and she quickly unbraided it. Swallowing hard, head held high, she walked out of the pool, pulling her loose hair over her breasts and using her hand to cover her quim as much as possible.

As soon as she was on the grass, Jane edged toward the bush where her clothes were. But one of the men, who wore feathers and decorative strips of curling hide in his hair, made a sharp sound. He shifted his spear, pointing it threateningly at her, and she stopped.

The man made another sound and jabbed his weapon at her again and Jane stepped back. He looked at Jonathan and said something, and his companions made sounds of agreement.

"Raise your arms," Jonathan said. "Jane, he wants you to raise your arms. They want to…see you."

"Jonathan," she whispered. "Do you know these men?"

"Do as they say," he said. "Please, Jane."

Slowly, she lifted her arms, and, following the motioned directions of the presumed leader of the group, placed her hands on top of her head. Her heart was pounding so hard her hair shivered over the tops of her breasts, brushing her belly and hips in a ticklish motion.

When the leader stepped toward her, Jane's breath caught and she had to bite her lip to keep still. She sensed that begging or talking or crying out would do nothing to help her and Jonathan. As the native approached, she felt his gaze scan her, heavy and intent. He kept his spear at the ready, but he had one hand free, and with that hand, he reached out.

Jane could hardly keep from rearing away, but Jonathan's hissed warning held her steady. The leader's hand touched her hair, sliding down over the curling golden-red locks, sifting it through his fingers. The wonderment in his face and expression was not what she'd expected, and something Jonathan had said to her previously popped into her head.

...with your pearl-white skin, blue eyes and hair the color of flames, surely they would think you a goddess.

Jane shivered as he stroked her hair over and over, as if to assure himself it was real. Then man took a large hunk of it, wrapping the curling locks around his fist. At first, she thought he meant to cut some of it off—he seemed so amazed by its unusual color. But instead, he lifted it away from her breasts and torso.

Now she was completely exposed, and as Jane stood there, her hands on her head, captured by her hair, the others stared at her greedily. Some of them edged forward, prodding Jonathan with them. When she attempted to turn away or raise her thigh to huddle down, the leader twisted her hair up sharply. She gasped and tears of pain sprang to her eyes as he pulled it high and tight. He said something and one of the other men came forward.

Jane tried to shrink away again, but the hand holding her hair had her immobilized and the spear touching her throat was an even stronger warning. The second man was more curious than the first, for he walked in a circle around her. She felt as if she were horseflesh being considered for sale, his eyes taking in every bit of her bare, trembling body.

When he touched her, a light finger down her spine, Jane jolted and cried out in shock more than anything. The hand grasping her hair yanked her back upright, bringing more tears to her eyes. Then the finger down her spine returned and slid into the cleft of her arse, gently and lightly tracing it down between her legs. Her quim pulsed in surprise and shock as another finger brushed over her labia.

She couldn't look at Jonathan; she couldn't look anywhere but into space. What were they going to do to her? Would they rape her right here, now? Or would they take her back… somewhere?

And what about Jonathan? Would they kill him or take him too?

Mercifully, the finger was removed after one brief touch. Then the second man, who had more paint on his face than any of the others, came around to the front of her. He stared into her eyes with emotionless brown ones, then his attention traveled down to her lips and breasts and the triangle of fiery hair at her thighs, then to her feet.

She braced herself, but instead of touching her again, he merely looked at the man who held her hair and gave a short nod, then spoke rapidly.

The next thing Jane knew, she was being prodded toward Jonathan. The man released her hair, but when she would have lunged into her lover's embrace, two warning spears blocked her.

"What are they going to do with us?" she asked Jonathan. His tension seemed to have eased, and his arms now hung at his sides.

He spoke to the natives briefly, and she wondered again whether he knew them or simply knew how to communicate with them. Was he negotiating their release?

He looked at her, some undefinable emotion shining in his eyes. "Jane. I don't know how to tell you this, but…they are taking us back to their village. We must go with them."

VIII

JANE CONSIDERED HERSELF FORTUNATE that the native men didn't bind her hands as they traveled. Perhaps they assumed their spears were enough of a threat. Or perhaps she and Jonathan weren't exactly captives as much as...guests.

A bitter laugh lodged deep in her throat as she traipsed through the jungle away from the hot springs pool. Guests? Guests were allowed to wear clothing, she assumed. But although one of the men gathered up her things, he didn't allow her to put them on. Instead, he merely raked over her with an appreciative gaze and gestured with his spear for her to walk.

The ground was prickly and rough beneath her feet, and it wasn't long before Jane felt the dampness of blood in her footsteps. Dear God, how long would they make her walk like this? Her feet would be in ribbons, and her skin would soon be sliced and scraped from the sharp edges of ferns and palm leaves.

Thus she was relieved as well as frightened when they reached a group of boats floating in a small river a short distance from the hot pool. The boats were long and narrow, created by hollowed-out tree trunks. Hers tipped wildly as she was forced to climb in.

Jonathan wasn't allowed to sit in her boat, and Jane's apprehension grew when she was surrounded by three men in her boat. If they were traveling by river, that would take them even further away from her father and Effie, and Kellan Darkdale. Even he wouldn't be able to track them.

A sudden hopeful thought had her looking up into the trees. *Zaren.* Could Zaren be up there? Watching? He always seemed to appear just when she needed him.

She peered up into the thick green canopy as the boats shoved off from shore, hoping and praying she would recognize some human movement. That he'd come swooping down from the trees and snatch her to safety. But it was dark and shadowy, and other than birds, flying squirrels, and other tree inhabitants, she could see little.

But Zaren had brought her back to her bedchamber secretly, with no farewell. Was that his way of discarding her? He had taken what he wanted—what she'd willingly given—and now he was finished? And even if he wasn't…what were the chances that he'd be watching at this very moment as she was spirited away?

Jane's thoughts spun and sifted thus as the boat sped swiftly down the river. For a small channel, it was rough and quick, and with every moment, Jane knew she was getting farther and farther from ever seeing Papa again.

Would he even notice? It might be best if he didn't, after all. She blinked back tears and tried not to think of what sort of grief he might endure, never seeing her again. She was glad, for once, that he was so intent on his work that he paid hardly any attention to the rest of the world. Perhaps it wouldn't be so bad for him.

Miserable and frightened, she made it through the day's journey. As the sunlight faded, the jungle became darker, and at last, they pulled the boat up onto a shore. If she thought they'd arrived at their destination, Jane was wrong.

There was no sign of a village or anything other than a simple clearing with the remnants of an old fire. The men made another fire while she was forced to sit and watch. They cooked and then fed her and Jonathan. She ate, despite not knowing what it was. Jane wasn't a fool. She knew whatever happened, she had to keep up her strength and wait for any opportunity to escape. She could follow the river back upstream and find her way back home if she had the chance.

If only she had some clothing.

The natives hadn't allowed her or Jonathan near each other, and any time she attempted to speak to him, he shushed her, looking apprehensively at their captors.

Although she'd been unbound all day, when it came time to sleep, the leader came over to Jane and tied her wrists together in front of her. He laid a blanket made from soft woven reeds on the ground and gestured for her to lie on it, which she did with some difficulty due to her bound hands. Then he tied her wrists to the base of a nearby tree, thus ensuring that she would be lying prone all night.

From her awkward position, Jane tried to crane her head around and see what they'd done with Jonathan. But he was out of sight and when she tried to move into a better position, a spear thrust into the ground in front of her and one of the natives glared down at her. Thus subdued, she sagged back onto the ground and tried to sleep, praying that there wouldn't be a snake or feline or some other wild animal that attacked their camp. She'd be ripe and ready for its dinner, all trussed up like this. She closed her eyes and forced herself to relax.

Jane awoke suddenly.

It was pitch dark. Even the fire had burned out. But someone was there, behind her. She tensed and gathered herself up to scream when a hand clamped over her mouth.

"Jane, it's me," Jonathan said in her ear.

Relief washed over her and her muscles slacked. "Thank God," she whispered. "Oh, thank God, Jonathan, you're free. Can you untie me?"

"Jane," he said, his mouth close to her ear. His body was close behind her, long and warm and comforting. "I can't. They're watching. They'll kill me if I try to free you."

"But Jonath—"

"Shhh," he said, and his hand slid around her from behind. He cupped one of her breasts as he pressed a kiss to her neck. "I know you're frightened. Everything is going to be all right." His tongue flicked out and slid into the soft, sensitive crease of her neck and she shivered.

"Jonathan," she whispered, but his hand moved back over her mouth before she could ask how he'd gotten free.

"You must be quiet, Jane," he said, his voice strident and directly in her ear. His fingers were tight over her lips, almost painful. "They'll kill me if they know I'm trying to comfort you. Now, relax. And let me comfort you, darling."

She realized with a start that he was rubbing a very insistent erection against her backside. Before she could react, he removed his hand from her mouth, whispering, "Don't make a sound, Jane. *You cannot make a sound.*"

She tried to move, but her hands were fixed above and in front of her, and she dared not speak again for fear Jonathan's threat would come true. If he were killed, what would happen to her?

He covered her breast again, finding the tender peak of her nipple. Jane closed her eyes, clamping her lips closed as he rolled the tip between his fingers, gently massaging it into a hard point. "Mmm, yes," he murmured duskily into her ear. "That's my Jane."

Little streaks of pleasure-pain jolted down from his fingerplay to her quim, and Jane felt her body begin to prickle and awaken. Her breathing quickened and she had to close her eyes, concentrating on not making a sound. His cock slid along the crevice of her arse, hard and hot, and she shivered when he buried his face in her neck, licking, nibbling, kissing along the sensitive skin there.

Then his hand slid down over the trembling skin of her belly, down to the coarse hair that grew between her legs. She shifted her knees apart, allowing him to find her swelling labia and the rock-hard sensitive pearl hidden there. He slid his hand, all four fingers, down and over the front of her quim, slipping through sleek and hot wetness, back and forth and back and forth until she wanted to scream.

But Jane kept her lips clamped shut, biting her lip, squeezing her eyes closed as the wide swath of his fingers teased and stroked over her nether parts. He moved against her from behind and she felt his breath on her shoulder, panting hard and hot into her steaming skin. Then he moved his hand, prying her legs apart from the front, clearly trying to keep his movements subtle.

His cock bumped against her from behind, then, after two poorly-aimed attempts, he slid inside. Jane's eyes flew open at the shock of pleasure, then she closed them again as he began to thrust. Holding her, one-handed, at the hip, he slammed inside her, fast and hard, all the while breathing hot against her neck, murmuring things she couldn't hear. His other hand gripped her extended arm, as if needing to stabilize himself as he pumped deep and hard inside her.

Jane gasped silently when she came, the effort of holding herself still and silent making the orgasm all the stronger. The strong shudders rippled through her body as Jonathan pounded into her one last time, then shot his release inside her.

She was still breathing heavily, still quivering, when he pulled away, silently and quickly. With one last kiss on the shoulder, he left her there, hot, sated, and just as confused as ever.

Jane was pulled to her feet the next morning after her arms were unbound. Staggering into the overgrowth, she relieved herself, wishing for the hot springs pool again. Last night's activities had done nothing to alleviate her aches.

She tried to speak to Jonathan, but once again was rebuffed before being forced back into the boat for what turned out to be another long day of travel.

But this time, when the boats finally pulled up on shore near the end of the day, Jane immediately saw that this was a permanent residence. Women stood in the river, washing clothing and collecting water. Smoke rose from above a low set of trees, where, presumably, their homes were arranged. Children played on the shore and other adult men came to greet the arrivals.

Everyone stopped what they were doing as Jane was ushered from the boat at spearpoint once again. If she'd been mortified by her nakedness before, she was even moreso now as dozens of pairs of eyes watched her. Men, women and children stared as she stood on the shore, thankfully, partly covered by her thick hair.

Her captors gathered around her and Jonathan, directing them to walk away from the river on a well-traveled path into the jungle. The ever-present spears accompanied them, surrounding them in front and behind, and the group was followed by the gawkers.

When they reached the village, Jane saw a circle of ten or more square-shaped huts made from grasses and bamboo. They looked like the drawings of native houses in Con Bellingsworth's book. One of the buildings was A-shaped, and smaller than the others. It was raised on low stilts and had steps leading into it. In the center of the circle was a large raised square, like a stage, and to the side burned a massive fire contained by a ring of stones.

As the group approached the village, more people appeared. They crowded around, speaking excitedly among themselves, pointing and gesturing to her and Jonathan.

At last, they stopped, and Jane was ushered up on to the stage-like dais by two of the spear-wielding natives. Jonathan remained on the ground, surrounded by their captors. She stood, looking up at the sea of faces, as the leader of her abductors spoke to the villagers.

To her shame and distress, he once again bundled up her hair and lifted it, forcing her arms up at spear-point. Jane stood on the stage, completely naked and exposed, her arms high, her breasts lifted, for all to see. Her captor forced her to turn in a slow circle to ensure that everyone could see her from every angle, and Jane fought to keep her chin up and her stance proud. If she had nothing else, she had her strength.

The audience made noises of jubilation and celebration and at last, she was allowed to relax. Then Jonathan was brought onstage with her, and the cries of jubilation and celebration became louder and more raucous.

She turned to him, surprised when her captor allowed her to rush over to her lover. Clinging to Jonathan, she said, "What is it? What's happening? What are they doing?"

He looked down at her, stroking his hand down her long, shimmering hair. "They've brought you back here to honor you, Jane," he said, smiling oddly. "They believe you're a goddess, a fertility goddess. Their desire is to please you and pleasure you."

"But…I…Jonathan! How do you know this? I don't want to be a fertility goddess," she said, trying to hide herself with his body. "I'm *not* a fertility goddess!"

He stroked the hair from her face and said, "It doesn't matter what you want, my darling. It matters what they believe. You must submit to them, to whatever they want. You must allow them to do as they wish, to pleasure you as they will. If you don't…they'll kill us."

Colette Gale

Dear Reader:

Welcome to the third volume of Miss Jane Clemons's adventures in the jungles of Africa.

If you have already read the first or second volumes, you need not continue with this introductory epistle, and can move directly forward to the first chapter. For those who have not read Entwined *or* Entangled, *please feel free to read on below.*

During the late 19th century, the British indulged in much exploration of Africa, searching not only for gold and gemstones, but also for knowledge of this fascinating Dark Continent.

Professor Everett Clemons, the famous lepidopterist, and his daughter Jane were two of the most famous British citizens to embark on these travels, and although Jane published a book of her drawings and notations about the butterflies her father studied during these trips, there remained little information about her own thoughts and adventures—until now.

Recently, I was fortunate enough to come across an old trunk filled with Professor Clemons's journals and butterfly specimens, and there, within, I also found the treasure of Miss Jane Clemons's personal journals.

Because there were so many volumes of her journals, I have chosen to publish a series of short segments over time in order to make them publicly available as quickly and efficiently as possible.

I do hope you'll indulge my decision to follow the popular form of literature from this era and publish Jane's journals as a serialized collection. And I must warn you: also in the tradition of the times, each episode ends on a cliffhanger.

The previous volume ended with a most unsettling event: the kidnapping of Jane and her fiancé Jonathan by members of a native tribe. They were taken to the tribe's village, where Jane learnt the natives believe she is a fertility goddess.

I hope you find Jane's adventures enlightening, exciting, and titillating as we follow her further adventures as a young woman in the Madagascar jungle.

Colette Gale
October 2013

The Jungle of Madagascar
1890

JANE STOOD on a dais above the small crowd of gawking tribal villagers. Unlike her naked self, they were all dressed in native clothing. Some wore feathers in their hair or on their revealing clothing, others had beads, woven bits of string, and what appeared to be small bones as decorations. The women wore short, shift-like dresses that ended just above their knees, while the men had fastened cloth around their waists. Some of them sported open, sleeveless waistcoat-like coverings over their torsos, decorated with stitching and feathers.

The color of the villagers' skin varied from ebony to light coffee with cream. But all of them had dark eyes and black hair that appeared springy and soft. And they were all looking at her with avid, hungry eyes.

Using the long, curling curtain of her fiery hair, Jane tried to cover her nudity as much as possible as she clung to Jonathan.

"They believe I am a fertility goddess?" Jane whispered to Jonathan, repeating his shocking explanation for their abduction of her and her fiancé.

She wasn't certain whether she was glad he could speak and understand the native language, or if she'd have preferred to remain ignorant of what was to befall her. No, that was foolish. Of course she needed to know. How else was she going to figure out how to escape? "What are they going to do to us?"

Jonathan was still clothed, but appeared no less a captive than she, for a spear was pointed at his chest, and another at his belly. His arm tightened around her. "I don't know, but I think we must do whatever they ask. I'll try to find out more information, Jane, but you must understand…they see you as a goddess. You are so different from them, they believe you must be divine. You must—"

"I must act like a goddess," Jane interrupted, suddenly seized with a rush of strength. Pulling out of his grip, she straightened her spine and stood erect, fully aware of the array of eyes on her. They were heavy and avid, the pairs upon pairs of them. More than a dozen, perhaps two dozen.

But if she were a goddess, she would stand proud and confident, for goddesses wielded power, did they not? Goddesses could bestow grace upon the people.

And above all, goddesses must not be angered.

Thus, she stood as tall and proud as she could force herself to be, completely naked and—for the moment—at the mercy of this tribe. Jane looked around with as much boldness as she could muster. She met the hot, needy eyes of the men and the curious, apprehensive gazes of the women as if she had the power they believed. The heavy heat of the jungle seemed to press against her bare, unprotected body, and the faintest skitter of a breeze brushed over her flesh. The ends of her hair rippled slightly and she could taste a hint of salt on her upper lip as she moistened it, aware of the sheen of perspiration on her skin.

Jane could only imagine how she must appear to the natives: tall and ivory-skinned with green eyes and high, generous, pink-tipped breasts. Her curls fell nearly to her waist, thick with soft waves, and fiery red-gold in color. It was no wonder they thought her a goddess, with hair such as hers. It was like a blaze. Like a fire.

Fahhr.

Fire.

Jane felt a sharp, unexpected stab of pain in her belly. *Zaren.* The wild and passionate jungle man had been gentle and reverent as he reached to touch one of her long curls. *"Fahhr,"* he'd said, his blue eyes wide and soft with awe. *"Fire."*

Zaren. A little quiver caught her by surprise, and then was gone, replaced by despair. She would never see him again. She couldn't, for even if—no, *when*; *if* wasn't even a possibility—she and Jonathan escaped from this situation, she would marry her fiancé and they would return to England.

Jane blinked hard and jolted back to the present when one of the presumed tribal leaders shoved Jonathan away and came to stand next to her. Her heart began to beat harder and her throat went dry as he gestured for another man to stand on the other side.

They spoke to each other, to Jonathan, and to her—though she couldn't understand anything they said—and then to the group of twenty-some people standing in front of the dais. The man in front of her had cold, dark eyes and he wore a woven red band around his throat.

Jane did not like the way he looked at her, and it took every bit of composure to remain silent, maintaining her haughty look even when he reached out to cup her breast. His dark, hot hand curved under it and he hefted it lightly, speaking and gesturing all the while. Jane couldn't understand his words, but the meaning was all too clear—particularly from his low, liquid laugh and the similar response from the audience. Her areola tightened, its nipple thrusting in response to the attention being given to it.

When Cold Eyes shifted his thumb to rub over the sensitive tip, Jane couldn't help but rear back a little, trying to put herself away from the unwelcome but erotic sensation. He made a sharp sound, and the next thing she knew, Jane's wrists were grasped by two strong hands from behind.

The man standing at her back forced her arms straight out from her sides, his fingers tight around her narrow wrists. He now stood so close behind her, she could feel the heat of his body…and the gentle brush of his loincloth, for it had lifted with his obvious erection. She swallowed hard and focused on a hanging vine in the distance, above the rapt crowd. Her guard's breath was warm and moist against her temple, and she could smell the man's essence—not unpleasant, simply unfamiliar and strange.

Those in the audience made a noise of satisfaction as she was spread out in front of them, her arms wide and helpless, extended from each side.

This gave Cold Eyes the opportunity to fondle each breast in turn as Jane stood still, trying to keep her breathing steady and herself from shrinking or trembling. *For Jonathan. And yourself. You are a goddess. They want from you. They want to please you.*

If only she could speak their language or otherwise communicate with them—to tell them if they didn't do what she wished, she would bring the wrath of all her powers down on them. How could she demonstrate this?

Then all coherent thought scattered as Cold Eyes slid his hand down the gentle swell of her belly and lower. Jane couldn't help but tense, unable to keep from twisting away as he approached her mound. Cold Eyes stepped back abruptly and made a sharp gesture to someone on the ground, and a tall, sleek, ebony-skinned man vaulted up onto the dais in a flutter of loincloth and a flash of muscular flank.

She might have admired his long, lean muscles and broad shoulders if she were anywhere but here. He flashed her a devilish white smile, and before Jane knew what was happening,

Devilish Man knelt in front of her.

As Guard One held her arms spread wide, the sleek newcomer forced her ankles apart…and apart…and apart. She fought to keep her knees together, but he was there—just in front of her belly. She felt the heat of his breath on her skin, and the strong, dark hands as they slid down her pale thighs to her knees, forcing them to move. The man behind her pulled Jane back so she was tilted off balance, making it easier for Devilish Man to have his way.

When her legs were open and her ankles spread to nearly shoulder width, Cold Eyes brought a spear forward. Jane tensed again, bracing herself for a blow or a stab or something… but instead, Devilish Man tied one end of the spear to one ankle and the other end to her second ankle, thus ensuring she couldn't bring her legs together again.

She felt the fresh, warm air on her quim, open and bare to whoever chose to look…or feel. And Devilish Man did just that as he finished tying the second bond, sliding both hands up along her outer thighs to the bush of fiery red hair, then bringing his face right into her pussy.

Jane jolted, gasping as he pressed his full lips against her labia, and she felt his tongue flicker out against the deep, hot folds of her. Cold Eyes made a sharp, angry noise, but Devilish Man took his time easing back and standing. He flashed her a hot smile as he rose and Jane's lungs felt as if they'd been constricted. The man's entire persona bespoke of devil-may-care insouciance as he turned, taking a second spear from one of the other tribal members.

Jane had no choice but to stand immobile as her wrists were lashed to the wooden pole, which rested over the back of her neck and along her shoulders. When they were finished, she stood in the familiar pose that appeared in Leonardo da Vinci's drawings, arms and legs spread-eagled in a large X-shape.

And then, just when she thought her current humiliation

was enough, two poles were brought forward and arranged on either side of her. Stronger and thicker than the spears, each was tied vertically from ankle to wrist, so Jane was in effect boxed into position.

A loud roar erupted from the audience as Cold Eyes gestured to her as if to say, *Behold! See what I have for you!*

He fixed her with that cold, arrogant look and approached, standing directly in front of her as Guard One and Devilish Grin flanked her on either side. Jane tensed, trying to keep her expression calm and empty as he covered her breasts with his hands, molding and stroking them roughly. Then he slid them down to her pussy, plunging both sets of fingers into her thatch of hair and stroking over her full, moist quim. Jane couldn't remain still, and she twisted and tried to shift away from those thrusting fingers—but she was helpless, for each of her guards held one of the vertical poles in position.

At last, with a sound of triumph, Cold Eyes withdrew his hands. The tips of his fingers glistened in the bright sun. He made a great show of smelling them, his eyes widening and his smile turning feral as he turned back to his audience and displayed them, slick with her juices, as if he'd acquired some great trophy.

Another roar came from his people, and then with a curt nod and a short, abrupt command, Cold Eyes gestured to Jane's guards.

All at once, she was lifted from the ground as the two men hoisted her up by the vertical poles. Jane stifled a startled shriek as she was raised aloft.

Her strong two guards held each pole just below the midpoint, which put her feet at the height of their shoulders. With careful steps, they made their way down from the dais amid the roars and whistles of the audience, and as Jane hung there helpless, they began to make their way through the cluster of people.

Hands reached for her, grabbing at her ankles and legs as the tribal members began to chant and sing. They clustered about, making it difficult for the guards to navigate through the crowd.

Jane closed her eyes and tried to be thankful no one could touch her—though it wasn't for lack of trying. Her perch swayed and dipped as members of the audience jumped up or bumped into her captors.

When her guards stopped moving, Jane opened her eyes to see them in the midst of the group. Cold Eyes stood on the dais just in front of them, and with a broad smile, he made a sharp gesture.

All at once, Jane was falling, face forward. She couldn't stifle the scream, and closed her eyes as she plummeted toward the ground, her limbs imprisoned, helpless to catch her fall. Then she abruptly stopped in midair, jolting from the ties at her wrists and ankles. When she opened her eyes, she found herself face to face with a myriad of people, looking up at her.

They had hot, dark, avid eyes, and they were less than an arm's length away…and she was suspended above them, just above their heads like a bird on a spit above the fire of the crowd. Her guards still held the poles above their heads, but now she was turned facedown as they paraded her through the crowd.

Her thick hair fell like a heavy curtain on either side, and the natives reached up to touch it, pet it, pull on it, brush it, smell it. Her breasts dangled just above their heads, but the hands could reach. They were grasping, pinching, slapping hands that touched her there, brushing her nipples and belly, and roved along her legs and hips and into the hot, musky hair at her quim.

Jane closed her eyes, for she couldn't bear to watch the desperate hope and lust in the faces as she was paraded over them. The chants grew stronger, undulating through the crowd, now followed by the dull, incessant beating of a drum. She tried to ignore the touching, petting, and stroking, but there were so many hands...so many of them...she couldn't block it all out. As hot fingers touched her, the sun blazed over her from above, cooking her buttocks and baking her along the length of her spine. Her wrists and ankles ached from the suspension, and her muscles strained and trembled as she hung in a gentle bow over the ground.

Jonathan. Where was he? Could he do nothing to help her?

What would they do to her now?

Her bold thoughts of strength and power slipped away as she realized just how helpless she was, goddess or no goddess. She had to talk to Jonathan. At least he could communicate with the tribal members.

And so why wasn't he trying to save her?

ZAREN PERCHED on a huge tree branch, surrounded by heavy foliage and hanging vines. A thick green snake slithered down the trunk next to him, and he politely moved so the creature could make its way toward its prey: the fist-sized red and blue frog sitting below.

Once the snake passed by, Zaren returned his attention to the den-like nest where he'd first seen the fire-haired woman named Jane. She wasn't there, hadn't been for two sunrises. Something inside his chest hurt, sharp and yet dull at the same time. Where could she have gone?

Settled on the branch, he looked through a large opening and watched the nest's current inhabitants. There were two of them, two creatures inside. Two just like him—with skin more pale than the other humans who lived in the jungle.

A *man*, he reminded himself, silently mouthing the word. *Woman.*

The two were mating…but in a way Zaren had never seen before. The man was sitting, and the woman climbed on *him*, spreading her legs, fitting herself over his rod, and embracing him from the front.

"Oh, Everett…darling…" Her moans wafted through the air, mingling with the rustle of leaves and the twittering of birds, the nibbling of some creature on bark or plants below.

Zaren could not take his eyes away from them. She was large and soft and round everywhere. Her damp skin beamed, white as the moon. Each of her amazing teats would overflow his hands if he cupped them together—something the equally round man was doing with enthusiasm as he kissed and licked the huge mounds.

The man's hairless head shone with perspiration, and even from where he perched on the branch, Zaren could scent the musky, titillating aroma of their activity. That smell, and the sounds, the sight of them rocking violently together brought back memories of Jane…of his mad thrusting into her glorious, wet warmth, of tasting her smooth white flesh, of burying his face in her sweet-smelling hair of fire.

"Effie! By *gad*, Effie!" cried the man suddenly. He sounded as if he were dying, or in distress. His head tipped back, his neck and arms strained, and his face was red with effort.

But Zaren knew better. That was no distress. He remembered the hot, glorious feeling of mating—and so did the heavy, pulsing rod that had risen between his own legs. His member was so tight and sensitive that it was painful to the touch, with a dull throb of need that could hardly be sated by the grip of his hand—and even then, only temporarily.

For every time he thought of Jane, and when he remembered her lovely eyes—the color of the sea beneath a cloudless blue sky—and recalled the way her skin had trembled the first time he reached to touch her, how reverent he'd felt, how awed by her beauty and taken by her scent, how kind and funny and patient she'd been when they were in his own nest in the trees…every time he thought of her, he grew short of breath, and hard, and his muscles tightened everywhere. And that dull ache inside his chest blossomed into something warm and fierce.

The first time he'd seen her, walking off the long branch from the…what was it? *Boat.* No, *ship*. He nodded to himself, remembering the pictures in the book, and how Jane had sat with him, practicing many of the words. His head didn't hurt so much anymore when he looked at that book. The words were coming back.

He was *remembering.*

As if awakening from a long dream, shaking off the last bit of sleep, he remembered. Knowledge, long buried, had begun to flood his mind; words returned, thoughts clarified.

And now, as the mating man and woman disengaged themselves from each other, he could hear them speaking. In low murmurs, punctuated with sighs and smiles.

But when the man said, "I'm worried about Jane," Zaren stilled and listened, every hair on his body lifting in recognition and interest.

Jane.

The woman was shaking her head in a way that made Zaren understand she was concerned too. "I don't trust that Mr. Darkdale, an' I'm not even sure as I trust Mr. Jonathan. Man disappears for three years and then returns all-a sudden… and now Miz Jane is gone too." Her yellow hair stuck out in tufts all over her head, but her eyes were filled with worry.

Jane. Gone.

Mr. Jonathan.

Zaren felt an odd, curling tingle in his belly. Jane had called a man Jonathan, the man whose sudden appearance in the jungle had caused her to faint.

He was the man who mated with her in the bubbling hot pool…and then allowed another man to mate with her as well—while he *watched.*

Zaren's body tightened with disgust and fury. If Jane were his mate, he would *die* before he allowed another to touch her. An unfamiliar, bitter taste filled his mouth as he remembered his first impression of Mr. Jonathan.

He wanted to maim him.

And now Jane was gone, and so was this despicable Mr.

Jonathan. And the mating man and woman—he wasn't certain if they were called Effie and Everett or Gad and Darling—were worried about Jane. They wouldn't be worried about her if she was safe, would they?

As the tuft-haired woman looked out into the jungle, right in his direction—almost as if she could see him—Zaren became as still as the bark of the tree. He knew how to meld into the sun-dappled leaves and vines, becoming invisible to prey and predator alike.

"Someone must find 'er, and bring Miss Jane back," said the woman, staring at Zaren's tree. "Get th' girl away from the snakes and bad 'uns in the jungle. Someone must bring the poor chit back to us, Everett. Someone must bring her home."

Zaren's heart pounded hard. Surely the woman wasn't speaking to him. Surely she couldn't see him…could she? Could she know he was there?

After one last look into the jungle, right at him, the woman turned away. But not before he saw her nod in his direction.

III

JANE WAS TAKEN to a small structure—a hut, really—and released from her bonds with surprising gentleness. Her two guards, Devilish Grin and Cold Eyes, helped her upright, their hands warm and absurdly reverent, except for when Cold Eyes skimmed a palm down the curve of her arse.

As Jane staggered to her feet, rubbing her scraped wrists, she gritted her teeth wryly. Of course they would be gentle with her. She was a *goddess*. Heaven forbid they anger—or injure—the goddess, she thought with an edge of hysteria. Jane pushed the thought away and straightened her spine.

"Jonathan," she said, trying to sound demanding and goddess-like. "Bring Jonathan to me."

He was her only hope. At least he could understand what their captors were saying, and find out what they meant to do. She had no way to communicate and little chance of understanding what was to happen.

You must do as they wish...for both of our sakes.

To Jane's surprise, her two escorts each gave her a deep bow and turned to leave the hut. "Send Jonathan to me!" she cried again, reaching for Devilish Grin's arm. He, at least, seemed friendly.

Perhaps too friendly.

He looked down where her pale fingers closed over his

dark arm, then allowed his attention to skim along her body, which at the moment was nearly cloaked by her hair. His eyes turned hot and he said something to his companion. They both laughed, low and lasciviously, and Jane dropped her grip immediately.

"My man," she said, desperate to make them understand. She gestured to the outside, trying to use hand signals to show she was speaking of the Englishman, the foreigner. "Jonathan."

Devilish Grin nodded, and hope rose like a burgeoning flame. If she could at least speak with Jonathan...

The guards went out of the hut, leaving Jane alone.

Blessedly alone.

She looked around the space. Though it was dim and small—hardly the size of a private parlor back home—she could make out what seemed to be a raised, thick-covered pallet in the corner. It was covered with furs and other, lighter material, and appeared almost comfortable—though anything would surely be comfortable after spending the night on the ground, tied to a tree.

A primitive, chair-like structure and a table were in the center of the room. The floor was made of hard-packed dirt, and the walls woven of dried grasses and reeds—just as she would have imagined a native hut in the jungle to appear. The roof was relatively high overhead, and in the corner was a small stone fireplace with a hole in the ceiling to allow the smoke to filter out. The faint glow of red told her banked coals waited for use, despite the oppressing heat of the jungle.

There was but one door and one window, which was covered by a woven mat and allowed very little light into the room. It was also on the side of the structure that faced away from the center of the village.

Heart in her throat, Jane went to the window. If she could climb out, perhaps she could run into the jungle and escape.

Trepidation seized her as she thought of being naked and

helpless in the thick, dark forest. She had no idea how far she was from camp, no concept of whether there was any other person around who could help her, what wild animals she would encounter…

Zaren.

She squeezed her eyes closed as they prickled with tears of frustration and regret. She imagined what would have happened if he'd been with her when the natives surrounded them…fantasized about him roaring with rage, fighting them off, flinging them weightlessly in all directions…then sliding an arm around her waist and launching them into the trees, gliding through the air on swinging vines. She remembered the feel of his warm body, the scent of his fresh, male skin and the brush of too-long but neatly coiled hair. And the slide of his bulky muscles, the delicate touch of his fingers as they smoothed over her skin…

Jane swallowed hard. She was in a fix—the worst predicament ever. Why was she daydreaming about the mysterious jungle man?

But she knew why he was in her mind—for somehow, she knew Zaren would never have allowed them to be imprisoned. He would never have allowed any man to put a hand on her.

Unlike Jonathan.

Jane allowed herself to wallow in misery and regret, then gave herself a sharp shake. So far, nothing utterly terrible had happened to her. Yes, she'd been paraded about naked…and she'd been touched and fondled…and *tasted.* Her quim gave a sharp, unexpected twinge at the memory of Devilish Grin's face buried in the thatch of her pussy hair, and the quick slip of his tongue.

But that had been the extent of her mortification. And there was still the window…

Jane went to the opening and carefully peered around the edge of its covering. Less like drapes than a simple shutter, the woven obstruction didn't fit completely…and there was enough space for her to look outside and see the figure of a man standing there.

Guarding her.

She wasn't going to be sneaking out any time soon. At least, unless she could find a way to distract the guard.

But even then, what chance would she have in the jungle, helpless as she was?

Just as the reality of her predicament sank in, the door opened. Jane whirled in a swirl of wild hair, her breasts bouncing, her heart thudding. But instead of Jonathan or Cold Eyes, or any of the other men—which, of course, was her greatest fear—a woman walked in.

She was followed by four other women, all—unlike Jane—fully clothed. They carried pots and cloths and other accoutrements, and Jane had a single wild thought of simply running past them, through the door, and tearing into the jungle.

But that, as Effie would say, would likely land her in the fire outside the frying pan she was already in.

"What do you want?" Jane asked, knowing they wouldn't comprehend, but still clinging to the hope she could portray some sort of control.

The first woman, a broad-shouldered, no-nonsense type, said something in return. Of course Jane had no idea what, but she stood tall and gave a regal nod. Then she gestured to the room at large, as if to give them permission to bring in their supplies. As each of the women entered and approached Jane, they gave a reverent bow, making a sort of gesture with their hands that was clearly a mark of respect—an absurd concept, with Jane being naked and the others fully clothed. But at least there was a measure of regard between them; perhaps she could somehow use it to her advantage.

By now it had become clear the women had brought the

necessary tools to bathe and groom her. Cloths and soft, woven fabrics that would be like towels, a carved-wood comb, jars and pots of substances that filled the hut with exotic smells, and a mass of bones, feathers, and shells that appeared to be a garment or some other adornment.

Last, there was a large woven object resembling a gigantic basket, brought in by four large men. At first glance, it looked as if the water inside would seep through, but upon closer look, Jane saw that the interior was lined with oiled, tanned hide. A bathtub.

The men—who ogled Jane appreciatively—were shooed out of the room just as they would have done back home in London. This was, clearly, women's work.

No sooner had the door closed behind the men than the five women took control, under the command of the broad-shouldered one. Jane's hair was bundled out of the way, and she was directed to the tub.

This she could understand—and was even used to. Normally at home, of course, she only had Effie to help her bathe and dress in the complicated, restrictive clothing of London—but to have five women seeing to her bath wasn't utterly off-putting, nor surprising, given her so-called goddess status. And very little communication was necessary, for they knew what to do and Jane—who was beyond exhausted—let them.

Perhaps, she thought half dreamily, sinking into the warm, scented tub, they would even allow her to rest and sleep after this.

Hands scrubbed her head, wetting her hair with a soft, creamy substance that smelled like tropical flowers. More hands attended to her feet, which were rested on the far edge of the tub. This basket-like container had soft edges and its sides were malleable, creating an extremely relaxing vessel in which to soak. Slick hands were everywhere, all at once—massaging and stroking.

As Jane tried to relax—to have her hair washed and then combed, to have her feet soaped and then massaged, followed by her arms, legs, torso, face, and neck—she drew in a variety of scents and smells. The hut seemed to have become warmer and closer, and a sleepy glance toward the corner told her the small fire was banked up. Someone had placed wide, damp leaves on the flames, and the resulting smoke wasn't unpleasant, but sweet and thick.

Her breasts floated just out of the water, warm from the rising steam, and her nipples pointed softly to the ceiling. Jane watched as if disembodied while two large, dark hands soaped and massaged them, brushing over each nipple once, twice, thrice, until she could no longer ignore the little zip of pleasure from the slick, warm strokes. Her breathing shifted and caught, and little frissons of pleasure mingled with the sure touch of hands, the soft lap of water, the dull, smoky essence in the air.

Then the hands moved to her arms, massaging them with the soft, sweet soap, and another pair of hands found her thigh and arse, lifting her from the bottom of the tub, massaging and rubbing as yet another pair of hands soaped her torso with the steaming water, and another rubbed her scalp and brushed her hair, then coiled and braided it. Each touch was impersonal—the women talked and chatted; even sang or chanted as they worked. It was only Jane who felt *every* touch, *every* stroke, *every* slide of skin over skin, until she realized her body was like one large, smoldering fire. She was full and soft and swollen.

When the broad-shouldered woman and one of her companions helped her to her feet, Jane stumbled, weak and lightheaded in a pleasant sort of way. *Sleep*, she thought. *If I could just sleep a little…*

Her long, damp hair brushed against her bare spine and arse, and the lightest touch of the hands directing her toward the pallet in the corner seemed to raise delicious sensations on her skin. The heavy, sweet floral and spice aroma filled her nostrils, clouding the room.

Somehow, she was on the pallet—a thick, soft, welcoming bed. Many hands lowered her reverently into place, and Jane's hair was tugged up from beneath her as she settled onto the softness. The fire glowed nearby, and the scent given off from burning leaves was even more pungent...and pleasant.

She turned to her side, curling up like a child to sleep, but firm hands directed her onto her back. Jane made a moan of protest, but there were too many hands to fight. Now new scents filled the air. Soft hands, slick with oil that smelled of flowers and other exotic scents, massaged into her clean, damp skin.

More hands settled gently over her throat, moving up over her jaw and face, and Jane drew in the beautiful, relaxing smells deeply. Whatever they were smoothing over her skin was delicious and heady, and her eyes sank closed. *After this, I'll sleep. I'll rest, and find a way out of here.*

But at this moment, even Jane didn't want to leave. It was heaven on earth: soft, warm, relaxing, and she felt as if her head and all of her worries had been sloughed away in the tub. For the moment, her world was sensation and pleasure and she no longer had the desire to fight it.

When her legs were drawn apart, Jane hardly noticed, for the long, smooth strokes on her calves and thighs loosened her muscles and brought gentle, tingling sensations to her skin. And there were hands at her torso, massaging her ribcage and beneath her breasts, and over her nipples, over and over and over...

Jane caught her breath as the languorous moment pulsed into a stab of pleasure. It shot in a little streak from her suddenly tight nipple down to her quim, where another pair of hands was very close by, rubbing oil into the inside of her thighs. She suddenly became very aware of hands on her breasts and nipples—three, or even four of them, massaging, fondling, sliding over the tight, sensitive peaks. The oil made everything slick and aromatic, and Jane's pulse bumped up as those hands slid and stroked, and her nipples rose harder and tighter, pleasure zinging down, down, down…to where someone was parting her legs even farther.

"No," she tried to protest, shifting her hips. But the hands at her thighs were strong and steady and they massaged and stroked that delicate curve of sensitive skin, right by her quim. She shivered, shifting, arching, her breath rasping and rough. Her little pearl pulsed and her labia swelled as if preparing for some erotic onslaught.

Hazy, yet fully aware of every touch on her body, Jane tried to push them away, struggled to prop herself up on her elbows. But she was too weak, too cloud-headed, and there were too many of them.

Dimly, she was aware of the women talking, looking at her, particularly at the bright thatch of hair between her legs. They seemed to be conferring about something, even as fingers stroked and—oh!—gave a little tweak to a nipple. Jane couldn't hold back a gasp of pleasure-pain and the women smiled with satisfaction.

One of them—the broad-shouldered one—nodded as if they'd come to some agreement. Jane, who'd been able to pull herself into a half-recline, was eased back flat on to her back. *Now what are they going to do?*

Her masses of hair were lifted and her arms drawn up into its heavy warmth. Jane was hardly aware of what was happening until she realized the women were *braiding her arms into her hair*. Like silken bonds, her long tresses were roped and braided around her wrists and arms, affixing her hands to the top of her head in a horrible—yet sensual—manner.

One of the women brought her a jug of skin, obviously thinking her thirsty, and lifted her to pour some of its contents down her throat. Water, infused with something fresh. It was crisp and cool and Jane drank even as she was aware of the women watching her. Waiting.

Someone had added more leaves to the fire, for the intoxicating, flowery, sweet scent filled the hut and Jane's protests fell away. Her thirst quenched, she lay on the pallet, her arms bound in her own hair, body glistening with scented oil.

Like a sacrifice.

Or a goddess.

Now the women stood around her, encircling the pallet. In the dim light, their eyes glittered with delight and heat. Expectation and anticipation fairly sizzled in the room. Jane opened her mouth to speak, but instead of words, the only thing that came from her was a sort of moan.

Then one of them—the broad-shouldered woman, the leader—bent over and placed a kiss on Jane's forehead…and then moved to press a kiss onto her lips…and then she moved to her chest, placing a light kiss on each shoulder, then into the curve of each underarm. Jane quivered, her breath unsteady as little prickles of sensation tightened her skin where the woman touched her.

When the leader came to her breasts, each up-thrust nipple received the same treatment: a kiss, moist and slightly longer than the busses pressed to her shoulders, and Jane couldn't control a sharp intake of breath. She tried to move, to shift away, but the broad-shouldered woman was strong and her hands fell to Jane's thighs, holding them down, pressing them wide open.

The other women were chanting something softly, and Jane found herself holding her breath as the broad-shouldered woman moved her hands, slick with the oil from her skin, down over her thighs, up and down, up and down…and then she knelt in front of her.

Jane moaned, her skin exploding with sensation and her insides with heat, but someone held her head and hands in place. She could see little, but she could tell was happening.

It was some sort of ritual, for the leader had placed several small bowls, burning with dried herbs or flowers, near the end of the pallet by Jane's spread legs. A new scent filled the air, and she saw a bit of smoke rising from the floor, seeming to mingle with the sensitive hair of her quim.

Then the leader knelt in front of Jane, who suddenly felt even more like a sacrifice...as if she were splayed on an altar and ready to be given to the gods.

She tried once more to throw off the imprisoning hands, but there were too many and they were too strong. Fingers closed over her thighs, and she submitted as purposeful thumbs drew her swollen nether lips wide. She felt the soft shudder of suction as they parted, felt the clinging moisture of her juices dripping free as her quim opened.

Spread wide, her pussy pulsed, hot and ready, and the broad-shouldered woman made a soft sound of delight or pleasure...then bent forward.

Jane jolted and gave a soft screaming gasp as the woman's mouth closed over her. Pleasure and shock bolted through her as the hot lips covered her swollen ones and settled there. Jane whimpered, shifting and shuddering, *wanting* something, waiting for something...and yet desiring to tear away, to break free and gulp in clean, fresh air.

The woman's mouth moved, and every brush of her lips against Jane's had her tensing and shivering, gathering up away and swelling, pulsing toward the heat of her mouth. Someone moaned, cried out softly in desperation, and Jane knew it was herself, unable to control the warring sensations of lust, pleasure, and denial.

The mouth covering her nether lips began to move, its tongue sliding out and slipping through thick juices, over pulsing, swollen flesh. Then she began to suck, to draw the little pearlish nub deep into her hot, slick cavern. Jane cried out loudly in shock and pleasure, and someone shouted from beyond—a man. One of the women swiftly covered her lips, stifling her moans and sighs as the hot mouth sucked and sucked and *sucked*...as if to taste every last bit of her.

Pleasure, hot and hard, shuttled through her body and Jane, smothered by a wad of cloth shoved into her mouth when she tried to twist away from the covering palm, bucked and rolled...trying to get away from the incessant stimulation—trying to find it and seize release. Her arms, bound up in her hair, struggled to free themselves, and the resulting pain at her scalp countered the intensity of the lower, lustful assault. The tongue played with her, slipping around without rhythm, sucking at the pearl and then slurping up the dripping, flowing juices, and Jane became nothing but an imprisoned, gasping, sweating pile of skin and bones, fighting and yet desiring—*needing*—release.

At last the woman pulled away, leaving Jane hard and full, wet, hot, pounding. The broad-shouldered woman's lips were swollen, shiny, and the scent of musk mingled with the incense in the air was pleasant and arousing. She smiled in satisfaction, looking at her comrades, and then using her tongue to lick away every last bit of musky essence from her lips.

Jane collapsed flat on the pallet, trying to steady her breathing, trying to disregard the intense throbbing between her legs. They were still spread wide, still open, and surely she glistened, fat and hot and red. If she could pull her knees together, press them tightly, she could find some relief.

But no. She was held in place and the chanting became louder. Jane tried once again to free herself, to spit out the wad of cloth in her mouth, but it was to no avail. The ritual continued.

Another woman stepped forward, pressing a kiss to Jane's

forehead, then to her lips, then her shoulders, her breasts…

Jane cried out from behind the cloth, knowing what was to come, and still, this hot mouth trailed down her belly, pressing reverent kisses all the way along the line from breastbone to pubis.

The chanting grew louder, the smoke thicker, the incense more cloying. Jane's skin seemed to burn; it was so hot, so full of *need.* Her body was tight and swollen and her entire being was focused on the fat, full, wet quim between her legs.

Please, she thought this time as the second woman settled there. Jane hardly knew what she was asking, but *please, please, please* ran through her mind over and over.

The lips pressed there, tasting, and the jolt of awareness over her swollen flesh was nothing more than a tease—a terrible, painful tease. The lips, full and soft and warm, were tentative—*too* tentative. Jane wanted to cry out when they bared brushed against her needy nether lips, her *desperate,* hot self…the core of her being.

A tongue flickered out as if to swipe up a taste, and Jane shuddered, hopeful, ready to explode into relief, and then the woman was gone, stepping back, leaving Jane's quim open, ready, and abandoned.

Tears of frustration and pain rolled from her eyes and Jane squeezed them closed. *What is this?* she thought as a third woman began the trail of kisses down her body. *What is the purpose of this?* To tease and taunt her into madness?

This time she tried to block it away, to cut off from her consciousness the sensations…hot lips closing over her painfully tight nipples…a sudden, unexpected tug at each one, sending a searing streak of lust down to her quim…a gentle brush of mouth over her quivering belly…the pressure of fingers against her thighs, holding her still and wide…then heat. Wet. Sensation.

The third mouth closed over her and all at once, a tongue

was delving wildly against her flesh. Jane's eyes flew open and she screamed behind her gag as shocks of hard, hot pleasure exploded over her.

Oh, yes, yes, yes...please...

The sucking, sliding, flicking drove her to a burning world of insane pleasure. She couldn't breathe, couldn't think—it was intense and painful and blazing with pleasure. The lips, sliding in her pools of juices, the tongue, flickering through every fold of her, then the sharp, hard sensation as her little pip was sucked and sucked and tickled and sucked...and everything shattered.

The red, rolling orgasm shuddered through her like a steam train, and Jane rose up off the pallet, gasping desperately behind the gag, her eyes rolling back into her head as she collapsed back down. Her scalp ached from her arms pulling her hair, and her breasts—heretofore mostly ignored—ached and jounced as she bucked.

She couldn't control her body as it continued to quiver and tremble. Pleasure still pulsed through her, juices dripped from inside her. The chanting had ceased for the moment, and her third tormentor had pulled away when Jane exploded. Now the women were speaking to each other, and Jane was dimly aware of their voices, hardly caring whether they seemed upset or pleased by this turn of events.

But no sooner had she begun to feel her body again than the chanting began once more, the heavy incense wavered forth more strongly, and the fourth woman pressed a kiss to her forehead...and then to her lips...and down, and down, and down...

Jane sobbed a little as the trail went inexorably south to where she was still hot and throbbing, still pulsing with tender little reminders of the previous onslaught. Her skin rose up in expectant little bumps beneath the soft lips of the fourth woman and she found herself tensing as the mouth drew lower and lower.

The barest touch on her nether lips sent Jane arching and moaning. The tongue, tasting her, swirling around and darting into her depths, sent strong, hot pulses through her. She swelled again, grew wetter, and the pleasure was so intense it was pain—pain that must have relief. Pain that mixed with slick heat and the sounds of lapping and licking, sucking and panting.

This mouth was incessant, drawing and sucking and stroking, until Jane felt herself climbing out of the pain and into the burn of lust. She trembled, feeling herself gather up again, tighten and throb beneath lips and tongue. Pleasure trammeled through her, building in that familiar way, and in the back of her mind she prayed that the mouth on her wouldn't stop… wouldn't *leave* her again…

Jane rolled and sobbed, heat and desire rising to a pinnacle… then exploded against the lips and tongue devouring her. She felt the mouth against her, drawing in the essence, the taste of her, the orgasm's juices, sucking and mauling as if it would never get enough.

And then, though she expected what would happen next—she'd be released, it would be the last time, the last mouth moving down on her—the unexpected happened. The fourth mouth didn't move. It remained there, licking gently, almost thoughtfully…darting a tongue in and out and around, torturing Jane's raw little pip back out into the depths of heat and wet.

Nooo…! she thought. *Noo…please, no more…*

But the mouth didn't release her, didn't leave, and the torture began again…

Jane could hardly think as her world flowed into the red hell of pleasure and pain, the incessant coaxing and teasing… more mouths, more lips and tongues, as if they meant to drink up every last bit of her goddess essence.

Orgasm after orgasm shocked her, some so hard they left

her crying…others exhausted and tiny…and still others sharp and tingling…

Until at last she slipped into a hazy world of nothing…of black-red nothing.

IV

JANE SLOWLY BECAME AWARE of her surroundings, opening her eyes to find that night had come. The memories of what had befallen her during the bathing session came flooding back, even before she realized she was, blessedly, alone.

Her heart pounding, she realized her arms were no longer bound, and that she'd been sleeping on the pallet completely unfettered and rather comfortably.

Comfortably…except for the dreams, which had been mingled with the hot onslaught of reality. Even now, her quim felt full and ready—even expectant—for another round of pleasure. The very thought made her cheeks heat with shame. How could she have responded to those women?

Perhaps I truly am a fertility goddess…a goddess of pleasure and coitus…

That thought made her feel even more confused, and she shook it away. Then, rising on unsteady legs, Jane looked around the hut. The fire still burned in the corner, but the haze-inducing leaves no longer smoldered in its coals. The lingering smoke was nothing more than common woodsmoke, filtering up through the hole in the ceiling. The flames there and in two small bowls set on the other side of the space gave off enough illumination for her to see that she was not only alone, but food and drink had been provided. And *clothing*.

Jane fairly fell upon the lightweight tunic, yanking it on over her head. The undyed fabric was woven of some surprisingly soft material, but even so, it brushed roughly over her sensitive nipples as she tugged it into place.

Once more modestly covered—at least to her knees—Jane turned to the food. Perhaps she could have peered out the window or door to see if she was still under guard, but a woman needed sustenance—especially if she was going to attempt to escape. And it had been almost a full day since she'd eaten.

Besides. She was a *goddess*. Surely a goddess was never left unguarded.

Her lips twisted at the thought, and Jane closed her eyes, pushing away the fear and apprehension that threatened to overtake her. If she became paralyzed by terror, she'd never escape.

The food was still warm—though not hot, so it must have been there a while—and was surprisingly good. Or perhaps it seemed so simply because she was ravenous. Some sort of tender, stringy meat, stewed with vegetables that must grow in the jungle. A bread-like substance, shaped like a round cake but perfect for sopping up the juices. Fresh fruit—some familiar, some more exotic, but all sweet, soft, and juicy.

Sweet, soft, and juicy...the words brought to mind her recent experience. She had, indeed, been thus at the hands—and mouths—of her attendants. Jane gave a little shiver, her cheeks heating again. They'd given her no chance, no choice but to respond. Between the sweet, drug-like smoke, the scented oils, the busy, insistent hands wooing her body with their touch...and of course, the lapping tongues and sucking mouths, she could not ignore the pleasure they gave her. Her little pip twinged in agreement, and as Jane bit into a soft pink fruit and the sweet juices exploded in her mouth, she considered her situation.

What occurred had definitely been a ritual, and the only explanation she could find was the women believed she was a goddess, and therefore believed she had some great powers. And what better way to obtain those powers, those abilities for themselves, than to partake of her…literally. What they'd done must also have been forbidden, for why else would they gag her to keep her silent?

Jane's mouth was dry and she felt lightheaded. That they meant to drink of her juices in order to reap the same benefits seemed obvious, if not appalling and darkly titillating at the same time.

And now that she thought back on it—which she could be forgiven for not having done sooner—she realized that of the people in the village, she'd seen no one under ten years of age. No children, no babies.

Apparently the entire clan was in need of assistance in procreating. She just hoped when they were finished with her, she'd be released, not made into a sacrifice of some sort.

The thought nauseated her and she rose abruptly. Time to see if she could take matters into her own hands. At the very least, she must see Jonathan. Perhaps he would know something more, have some idea how to escape this place.

As before, Jane peered out the edge of her window covering. Sure enough, a man stood there, staring into the night. To her dismay, he seemed wide awake, for every so often, he paced a few steps then turned and walked back.

It was even less likely she'd find an opportunity to leave through the door, but, though weak-kneed and still quivering randomly, Jane was determined. At the larger opening, she managed to pull away some of the grasses woven into the bamboo frame and made a sort of eyehole. This gave her another idea—one that made her heart bump in excitement—but first she had to see what was out in the front of the hut.

Through the small hole she could see the blazing fire pit in the center of the village. It must be very late, for there weren't many people standing around it, and the stars were high and bright in the sky. The forbidding jungle enclosed the small collection of huts, and Jane was once again reminded of the dangers that lurked within.

Escaping into the night, especially without a weapon, would be foolhardy at best.

Then she recognized Jonathan's tall, slender figure standing near the shadows, only a few feet from her hut. He seemed to be deep in conversation with one of the tribal members; their voices floated in bits toward her.

The other man shifted and his face became illuminated by the fire. Jane recognized him as Cold Eyes, the one who seemed to be the leader—and the one who'd touched and fondled her brazenly in front of his people. The one with the flat, lascivious smile.

To Jane's surprise, Jonathan wasn't bound or restricted in any way. And as they talked, she saw Cold Eyes give something to her fiancé. Something like a parchment or a rolled-up piece of skin. Jonathan nodded, satisfaction evident in his demeanor. He unrolled the item and looked at it, then glanced up at Cold Eyes.

Jane felt weak as she watched through the peephole, disregarding the irritating tickle-scratch of the dried grasses against her face. What was he doing? What was this about? Something didn't feel right. Jonathan was supposed to be a prisoner too.

You must do as they say, for both our sakes. Or they will kill me. Wasn't that what he'd told her?

Straining hard, hoping to hear some of what they were saying, Jane pressed her ear to the hole. Her heart thudded so loudly it nearly masked the sounds outside...but now she was able to hear unmistakable snatches of conversation. In

English. She could hardly breathe, and clung tightly to the door, listening with all her might.

"...brought her to you..." That was Jonathan; she recognized his clipped British voice. "...kept my promise..."

"...woman...indeed a prize..."

"...cannot tell anyone...release..."

"...map...Darkdale..."

"No, he does not..."

Jane had gone cold and numb. If she were a more fragile person, she would have collapsed in shock and horror. Her heart pounded in her throat, choking her with its force, and nausea surged, threatening to spill her recent meal on the dirt floor.

She'd heard enough. Heard and comprehended enough to understand. Jonathan had *brought* her here? Pretended to be captured and in danger? But he had *given her* to these people... for *a map*?

Her breathing became short and fast, and Jane spun back into the hut, looking for something that could be used for a weapon. Something. Anything.

With a roar of fury borne of deep, dark pain, she found a wrist-thick stick still burning in the fire. Yanking it free, she turned toward the door just as it opened to reveal her guard—presumably to investigate her shout.

Jane was so incensed, so blinded by rage, she swung the flaming stick at the man in the doorway. He was taken by surprise and stumbled out of the way as she burst out of the hut.

"Jonathan! You *foul*, lily-livered, dog-licking *snake*!" she screamed. She managed only a few steps before several hands grabbed her, pulling her up short, and yanked the flaming stick from her hands.

She kicked and fought, bit and screamed like a wild woman; all she wanted was the chance to kill him. To maim and torture him.

To destroy the man who *was supposed to love her*.

Jonathan, for his part, leapt behind Cold Eyes when Jane first came into view, but once she was subdued, he stepped back around.

"Jane!" he cried as she snarled and hissed, determined to get to him.

"How could you? Why would you ever do such a thing?" she screamed, fighting, kicking, even vaulting up so her legs came off the ground, cycling furiously in the air in his direction as she was held up by her arms. Thick curls flew in her face, tangled around her arms and shoulders. Tears rolled down her cheeks, and her voice was raw with grief and sharp from pain. "Jonathan…"

At last, she collapsed into the imprisoning hands, still sobbing with fury, shaking with a rage so deep she thought she might never find peace again. Hatred burned in her eyes as she looked at him.

"Jane, I'm…I'm sorry. I—"

"Be off with you," ordered Cold Eyes in stilted yet surprisingly good English. So he had understood her all along. His gaze glittered as he turned to look at Jane, hot appreciation burning in his eyes. "She will injure herself. But she is right. You are a snake. And she is a most magnificent woman."

"But…I can't leave *now.* It's night…and the jungle…" Jonathan stammered, his face suddenly glistening with perspiration.

"Go! You have what you came for. You are no longer welcome here." Cold Eyes made a sharp gesture and two of his men stepped forward with crossed spears.

As Jane watched, a combination of horror, rage, and grief fought inside her. With Jonathan gone, there was no one else here from her world. She would be utterly alone.

But she couldn't bear to set eyes on him—this man who'd

betrayed her in so many ways.

Yet if he were sent into the jungle at night, surely it would be a death sentence.

"No!" she cried suddenly. "Let him stay. Send him away at dawn. At least then there will be no blood on my hands...or yours."

Cold Eyes looked at her with consideration. "You dare to counter my command?"

Jane drew her aching body upright, ignoring the twinges and discomfort. It took great effort, but she managed to lift her chin into a haughty expression. "I am a goddess, am I not? You do not wish to anger me."

The tribal leader's expression blazed. "You are indeed some sort of goddess. And I shall soon find out just how much power you do have." Jane's insides wobbled unpleasantly at the unmistakable promise, but she held her head high as Cold Eyes turned back to his men. He spoke in their language, and the crossed spears fell away.

Jonathan surged toward her, but Cold Eyes stopped him. After he gave another short, sharp command to his men, Jonathan was led off and taken out of sight. As they took him off, he tried once more to look over his shoulder and call out to her, but she turned away, horribly disconcerted by Cold Eyes's promise and the fact that she was now utterly alone.

"Now, goddess," he said, taking her firmly by the arm. "Let us see whether I have made a good trade or no."

Jane's insides surged as he led her, not to her small hut, but to a larger structure. She stumbled, trying to slow his pace, trying to delay while she thought of a way to escape, but Cold Eyes merely gripped her harder and shoved her along roughly.

When they reached the building, which was about twice the size of her hut, Cold Eyes spoke sharply to the man who stood in front of the door. The guard hesitated, then reluctantly stepped aside as he opened the door.

Cold Eyes released Jane. "After you, goddess."

She had a fleeting moment of insanity and almost bolted, but that would be futile, and could result in punishment or worse. Jane knew she must marshal all of her courage and intelligence if she were to find a way to escape. The niggling fact that she'd been able to pull apart the dried grasses that made up the door—and the walls—of her hut gave her hope. If left alone long for a while, she was certain she could make a hole large enough to slip through and escape.

Eventually.

But now…

Jane looked around at her new environment, and immediately recognized its purpose. It was not, as she'd supposed, the home or habitat of the tribal leader.

No. It was some sort of temple or worship space. For some reason, that realization made Jane even more nervous—especially when she noticed an altar with what looked like arm and leg restraints.

Her heart pounded so hard she thought she might vomit. Jane drew in a deep breath and realized the space was permeated with a musky, dull scent of spice and some other unidentifiable aroma. While it wasn't exactly displeasing, nor was it particularly pleasant. Candles made from empty coconut shells lined the room, casting dancing yellow light on the grass walls.

"Goddess." Cold Eyes had come in and closed the door behind him. As Jane watched, he placed a large, heavy wooden brace against it, ensuring no one would be able to enter.

What was he going to do to her?

Her heart in her throat, Jane edged away from him, nearly tripping over a stool, then bumping into a table as she staggered away. The crude jars and vessels on the table clunked into each other, and Cold Eyes pinned her with his dark, hot gaze.

"What an excellent idea. Pour yourself a drink from the tall jug. And one for me as well."

"How long have you known English?" Jane managed to say, her hand shaking as she poured. A dark, thick liquid splashed into their bamboo cups. "You speak it well."

"I learnt it when I served as a groom for a regiment of your kinsmen's army, when they came to fight the Berbers." He took the cup and drank heavily, then gestured that she should do the same. "It will make things much more pleasant," he said with a cool smile. "For both of us."

The liquid tasted like bitter, fermented coffee, and was thicker than cream. There was a strange aftertaste that lingered on her tongue, and Jane realized it was likely some sort of hallucinogenic.

"You are in need of a drug to be with a goddess?" she taunted, then immediately regretted her bold words.

Cold Eyes's smile thinned, and anger flashed in his gaze. "You are a brave one. Perhaps you *are* the one woman who can—" He stopped abruptly, and his expression changed to a determined one. "Take that off. I will see all of you."

"You've already done so." Jane made no move to follow his command. She didn't know how or why, but something had emboldened her. Perhaps it was knowing she had no one on which to rely but herself now. Perhaps it was because she didn't believe they meant to kill her, or even hurt her. Or perhaps she was merely foolhardy, and the drugged drink was making her act thusly.

All at once, the thought of Zaren popped in her mind. *Zaren.* Jane felt weak at the memory of him, and at the same time, she had a brief moment of happiness. With Jonathan exposed for the vile man he was, she no longer must be conflicted between loyalty and…lust? Desire? *Love*?

Whatever she felt for the wild jungle man Zaren, though she might never have the chance to act on it again, at least she no longer must feel guilt or confusion about him.

If I ever escape from these people, I'll find Zaren. A warm, comforting quiver shuttled through her. *Oh, yes. I'll find him.*

And that thought, that bright light of hope, filled her mind as Cold Eyes grabbed her by the front of her tunic and shoved her back, back, back…until she felt something behind her thighs.

The altar.

Jane held to the thought of Zaren—his gentle, tender touch, his powerful sleek body, his kind, hot eyes—as Cold Eyes forced her back onto the flat surface, holding her by the throat. Her windpipe thus muffled, she could hardly breathe. Lights and black spots danced before her eyes, and she had no strength with which to struggle as her captor forced one wrist, and then the corresponding ankle, into the buckle-like restraints.

He finished by attaching her other wrist to the bound one, crossing that arm over her eyes. Spreading her legs wide, he pulled her roughly into place so that her hips and arse were positioned at the very end of the raised table. She was restrained there, precariously at the edge with its sharp angle digging into her buttocks, ankles and knees spread, her tortured red quim open and ready. Even now, she felt a soft little pulse of awareness from her tight little pip.

There was a change in the room; she could hear him moving around, felt the change in the air, the shift of scent. He was moving around her, chanting softly to himself.

After a long moment in which she wondered if he meant to simply leave her like this, he spoke. "Now then." Cold Eyes's voice sounded strained and a little high. "It is time."

Jane jolted as two hands closed over her breasts; she could see nothing, for her arm was crushed against her eyes. But she could hear his heavy, rasping breathing and feel the heat of his presence as he stood between her legs.

He toyed with her nipples, massaging them, rolling them

between his fingers until they drew up tight and close. Little tugs of pleasure jolted down to her belly, and turned to a sharp pulse when he closed his warm, wet mouth over one of her breasts. Jane couldn't hold back a gasp as he sucked hard, *harder* and longer, as if he meant to fit all of her into his hot mouth. She moaned when her pearl pulsed automatically in response.

Cold Eyes's breath became raspier, and he turned to her other breast, pinching and sucking until Jane could stand it no more and arched, digging her buttocks more sharply into the edge of the altar, trying to find a way to launch herself from the sensation…or to find some pleasant ending.

"No…" she moaned. "Oh, please…"

"That's it," he muttered. "Beg."

She felt him between her thighs, his hands gripping the tender skin there, and Jane held her breath, bracing herself to be filled. She tightened and panted, somewhere between apprehension and need.

He pressed against her—she felt the heat, the roughness of hair…and softness. Soft, squishy *something*, pushing against her swollen, sensitive quim.

Jane's eyes flew open beneath her arm as she realized what was happening. Cold Eyes smashed himself into her, pushing the head of his cock—a cock that felt as soft and useless as a worm—against her. He rubbed and manipulated, pressing into her wetness, sliding around and against her juices, trying to force it into place.

Jane couldn't ignore the pressure, the erotic slip and slide, and even while she understood her tormentor's predicament, she felt her own frustrated need rise as he massaged against her in an ineffective, tortuous tease.

He growled under his breath, something furious and tight, and she felt the tension in his fingers as he continued to hold her thighs in place. One hand released her leg and she felt him move against her, then the sharp motion as he attempted to jerk himself into an erection. She could hear the angry sounds of frustration, gasps of desperation, then suddenly he began to tear at the restraints on her ankles.

Jane's legs jolted free, and the next thing she knew, he flipped her roughly onto her belly in a swirl of hair. Her arms were tangled, her curls caught painfully beneath her, and the bonds loosened the positioning of her wrists so she could see the dirt floor just below her, while the rest of her vision was obscured by the rest of her hair. Her breasts dangled just over the edge of the altar, swaying and bouncing with his forceful movements.

With rough hands, he shoved her into place, spreading her legs so that her quim rested snugly against the flat surface. She throbbed against it, somehow her arousal even more pronounced when smashed against the altar. His moans of frustration were mingled with gasps of air and curse words that could only have come from his days with the British Army.

Grasping her hips, he pushed and rubbed his flaccid cock against her, sliding it along the crack of her arse. Jane shifted, stifling a groan as she was pressed into the table, trying to grin her needy, swollen pip onto the surface. She could hardly breathe from behind the thick curtain of hair that fell over her face, tickling her skin.

Just then, a loud noise came from outside. Jane heard shouts, and the hut walls shook as someone slammed into them—or, more likely, the door. Hazy with confusion and arousal, Jane tried to look through her hair toward the entrance as Cold Eyes sprang away from her as if burned.

He shouted something in his native language, and Jane recognized apprehension and something akin to mortification in his tones. Then he added something angrier, stronger, and she felt the air swirl as he went to the door—which sounded as if it were shuddering and bowing in its place.

The door opened—whether by Cold Eyes or not, she

couldn't tell—and more men came in. They were angry, accusing, and the group of them descended into an argument. She couldn't tell precisely what they were saying, but she got the impression that Cold Eyes, though he was tribal leader, had somehow overstepped his bounds—and he, in turn, was desperate for the others not to know of his deficiency.

For it had become clear to Jane why he, in particular, was in such need of a fertility—or in his case, sex—goddess.

Whatever they were arguing about seemed to be resolved quickly, for the voices settled into more civil tones. The air in the hut moved; she couldn't see any of them, or tell what they were doing, but it seemed as if some or all of them were leaving. *Leaving!*

And there she was: belly-first on the altar, her full, needy quim rosy and bare, her full breasts dangling, her arms and legs trussed too tightly for her to move to a comfortable position. She couldn't see anything but the floor directly below her, and although until now she'd been silent, Jane wasn't certain if they meant to leave her like this…and whether she dared chance drawing attention back to herself.

But who could ignore the image she must make?

The door closed and the bit of fresh air that had been wafting in ceased. *They'd left her!*

Before she could decide whether to cry out or try to free herself, the door opened again. A pair of large, dark-skinned feet came into view beneath her face. Whoever he was, he didn't speak. Instead, he moved to the side of the altar. An arm slid around her torso, gathering her breasts up into an embrace, mashing them back up against her chest. His hand cupped her far breast, gently sliding over the taut nipple there. He pinched gently, rolling the jutting tip between his fingers. Jane shifted, her breath quickening as he fondled her, and then abruptly, she felt something probing her slick, swollen quim.

A finger. Jane froze, holding her breath, as he slipped a

finger around her opening…and when he slid it home, all the way in, she couldn't control a gasp and a little pulse around him. Pleasure sang through her veins, centering and circling down to the full, wet center that hugged his finger. He slid it slowly out then back in again, and Jane quivered, shifting against the altar in an attempt to angle him deeper.

Tight with arousal, she clamped herself around the finger, and whimpered when he withdrew, aching for more…then gasped when two fingers slid in, and then three…

Tears ran from her eyes as he filled her with those three digits, sliding them in and out, faster and faster. Jane moaned and shifted, her quim dripping and swollen. The sounds of slick suction and the scent of musky juices filled the air, mixing with his rasping breathing and her own panting sighs.

"Oh…yes," she whispered. "Oh, please…"

Her body tightened, swelled, and then suddenly exploded. Jane cried out in relief as the hard-fought orgasm surged through her. His fingers continued to move, slipping wildly in and out of her tight sheath as she shuddered and trembled against the table, coming in one long, undulating ride of pleasure.

At last, he withdrew completely and released her breasts. Jane sagged, gasping, her body still pulsing in slow, dull waves. Her pip was big and full, pressed against the firm surface, still throbbing weakly as those large feet came back into view.

With quick movements, he loosened her ties, flipping Jane onto her back slightly more gently than Cold Eyes had done. She was still bound, but loosely, and her legs remained spread as he faced her. Her breath caught, for she was sure he meant to fuck her now. Her body drew up in anticipation once again.

Panting, Jane looked up to see Devilish Grin, gazing down at her with an expression filled with heat and something like mischief. His erection made a huge bulge beneath his loincloth, and when her eyes went there, he flipped the fabric aside. His rod sprang free. It was the largest, darkest, thickest cock she'd ever seen.

"*Oh*!" Jane snatched in her breath, her quim surging hot and wet in expectation. But Devilish Grin merely raised his glistening hand—the one that had slid up inside her—and, eyeing her with a hot, heavy expression, he eased one finger into his mouth. She shivered as he sucked on it, watching as his cock quivered, a drop glistening on the end of its massive length. Jane could hardly swallow. She suddenly wanted nothing more than that huge cock inside her.

He finished the first finger, then slid in the second one between his full, red lips, sucking on it, swirling his thick, red tongue around it as Jane watched, lightheaded and needy once again. She panted in short little breaths, damp and hot everywhere, as he licked all of her juices from each finger while that tempting cock teased her…just out of reach.

And then, his expression filling with bold promise, Devilish Grin bent forward to press his face into her quim. Jane nearly shot off the altar at the light, teasing touch of tongue…just at the tip of her little bud.

Shockwaves jolted through her, and her sensitive little pip pulsed with erotic pain…and then he stepped back…stepped *away*…and left her alone.

Hot, wet, and swollen.

ZAREN LIFTED HIS FACE and sniffed the air again.

Yes, that was it—the scent he recognized. A surge of hope leapt in him as he quickly climbed lower to the ground, disturbing a group of palm-sized orange birds as he descended the thick trunk of a tree.

For a day, he'd been following the trail—the scent, the footprints, the movements—from the nest where Jane and her friends lived, but then it was gone. A small river cut through the jungle near the area he lost the trail, and Zaren knew she must have gone somewhere in a boat. What disturbed him the most, however, was the clear signs of struggle that were left in the area. At least six men had been there, and Jane and her mate as well.

Gad and Darling were right: something bad had happened to Jane.

After losing the trail late before sundown, Zaren searched frantically through the night, taking only an hour of rest on two different occasions. He traced the jungle along the length of the river in search of some sign, some lingering smell that would tell him where she'd been taken. And finally, just now, he'd at last found something: a familiar smell.

Not the one he'd hoped for, but at least he had found something.

The scent grew stronger as he drew nearer the base of the massive tree, his strong feet curling around the uneven segments of bark that acted as steps.

It wasn't Jane's scent that he followed, but that of the man. Jonathan was his name.

Zaren knew if he found Jonathan, he would find Jane.

A rustle in the jungle below had him pausing to listen. It was a two-legged creature, making an awkward, fumbling noise. A man with little skill at moving throughout the jungle.

Curling his lips in a determined, feral smile, Zaren launched himself to another tree, catching a thick vine in the process. He swung silently and smoothly from branch to branch toward the sound, avoiding a massive brown spider that he knew had a dangerous bite and the particular bulbous green growth on a branch that would turn his skin red.

Zaren saw the thick greenery moving below, and with one last swoop, he landed in a branch above the man, then dropped neatly to the ground in front of him.

Jonathan staggered back in surprise, his eyes wide and arm upraised to shield himself. But once he recovered from the obvious shock, he straightened and whipped out something sharp and silver. Half crouching in front of Zaren, the pale-skinned man gave off the stink of fear mingled with determination. He waved the weapon in front of him and said, "Get back!"

"Where is Jane?" Zaren demanded. He'd practiced saying those words to himself, over and over, and now he spoke them with more confidence than he'd spoken any words as long as he could remember. "*Where is Jane?*"

"Who the bloody hell are you?" Jonathan replied, still brandishing his weapon. *Knife*, Zaren reminded himself. *Knife.*

"*Jane.* Where is Jane?" Zaren said again, eyeing the blade while keeping watch for any tension on the other man's feet and body. Jonathan appeared skilled with his weapon, and

Zaren remained on guard, as he would be when facing any wild animal. He would not underestimate this creature any more than he would a hungry lion or a coiled snake.

"Jane's gone," Jonathan said, but Zaren didn't miss the way his eyes flickered oh-so slightly in the direction of tonight's moonrise. "I don't know where she is."

Liar. The weak man in front of him spoke nothing but falsehoods, and Zaren read him as easily as Jane had read his picture book. Fury filled him, dark and quick, and his hand shot out with the speed of a snake's strike. He had Jonathan's wrist in his fingers in a trice, the knife falling harmlessly to the ground.

"*Where is Jane*?" he said again. This time, Zaren punctuated his demand by whipping Jonathan around by the arm, slamming him into a tree.

This knocked the breath out of the other man, but Zaren had no sympathy. He kicked the blade into the thick brush as Jonathan squealed, "My knife! I need my knife!"

"Tell me…where is Jane?"

"She's…she's…they have her. I was going to send for help when I got back. I was going to get Darkdale, and we were going to bring help." Jonathan's eyes were wide and pleading. "They made me leave. They have her."

Zaren dredged the word from deep in his memory, from some long-lost time: "Bastard." He tightened his hand around the man's throat. "Where?"

"That way." Jonathan pointed, then babbled out more information. His words were too fast and ran into each other as if they too were terrified—but Zaren only needed the direction. Now he could follow the trail the white-skinned, cowardly man had made when he left behind his mate.

Jane. Zaren would *never* leave Jane.

He would die before he abandoned her.

The very thought made his vision burn red and dark as he

looked down at the cringing man before him. "You leave Jane," he growled. "You *leave* her."

"No, no, they made me go, they sent me away. They won't hurt her."

Zaren had heard enough. With a roar, he flung the insulting weakling of a man away, tossing him into the brush with a great heave.

And then, without another thought for the man who'd left Jane, Zaren leapt up into the lowest branch of a tree and went to find her.

NOT LONG AFTER Devilish Grin left her sprawled over the altar, two women came into the room and took Jane back to her hut. Blessedly, she was then left alone and unrestrained, and she sank wearily onto her pallet. Her eyes closed readily.

Despite her apprehension about what was to come, Jane slept for much longer than she expected. When she awakened, the sun was already past its high point in the sky. Food and a jug of herb-scented water had been brought in some time during her sleep, and she ate and drank gratefully.

Her body was sore.: her wrists and ankles, while not horribly chafed, had red marks around them. Her muscles ached from being strung up on the spears and carried over the crowd, and her arms in particular screamed with pain every time she shifted.

But the worst was the sensitivity of her quim. Jane could hardly move without her legs brushing together, compressing her swollen nether lips and engorged pip. It seemed as if all the pleasure she'd taken the day before only caused her body to want more—to *need* to be touched, licked, sucked, kissed.

Jane had always enjoyed coitus, and been easily aroused, but her current situation was nearly unbearable. The constant throbbing and slick slide between her legs kept her in a constant state of arousal.

Did they somehow make me this way, or was I always a sex goddess? she couldn't help wonder, only partly in jest. Then even that bit of levity eroded into despair. *I must get away from here!*

Now, rested and her hunger abated, Jane had the opportunity to put into play a half-formed escape plan. She went to the farthest corner of the hut, the side of the structure that had neither window nor door, and that partly faced the jungle, and began to examine the wall. Made from dry grasses woven together with bamboo, the barrier to the outside was relatively flimsy.

It wasn't difficult for her to find a thin area of the wall, and to start pulling the grasses away, little by little. The trick would be to loosen it without making a hole until she was ready to go. And she wouldn't be ready to go until she had clothing, a skin for water, and some sort of weapon.

But at least she was doing something. Something that kept her mind off Jonathan and his grand betrayal, and something that kept her focused on her Papa and Effie, and the hope that she would soon see them again…and Zaren.

Jane paused for a moment, for the pain arcing through her heart shocked her. And despite the fact that her body cried for pleasure and a man's touch, it wasn't the thought of Zaren's strong, powerful body sliding against hers that made her insides hurt. It was his kind, brilliant blue eyes—filled with wonder and tenderness. And the reverence and joy with which he treated her, as if she were a prized possession, yet not a fragile one, to be protected and locked up in corsets and confined by heavy skirts. Despite their clumsy method of communication, Jane felt as if Zaren understood her in a way no one else did—accepting her for just what she was; no more and no less.

No man had ever looked at her in that way before, or treated her with such respect—except for Papa, on the rare occasions his mind wasn't wandering off to butterfly mating.

I will escape. I will find my way back...

Jane returned to her work with renewed fervor. Her fingers became scraped and raw from the dry, prickling grass and the sharp edges of bamboo, but that discomfort was nothing compared to the need that drove her.

Fortunately, Jane heard her captors approach before the door opened, and she had time to dive across the small hut onto her pallet. She was lying there when Cold Eyes walked in, followed by the five women from yesterday's bathing episode. Behind them were three men carrying the tub.

"Your bath, goddess," Cold Eyes said.

Jane couldn't control the little shudder that rippled through her at the sight of the women, and the memory of their pleasurable assault. *Please, not again...not again.*

But today's process was much different than that of yesterday's—and Jane attributed it to the fact that Cold Eyes remained in the hut, watching over the women as they bathed her once again. Perhaps he had learnt about the events of yesterday, and he didn't mean for them to be repeated.

Today her hair was kept dry, bundled onto her head, and the hands that soaped and massaged her exhausted body were, if not completely impersonal, at least not quite as invasive and erotic as before. But Jane couldn't ignore the knowing, heated look the leader of the women gave her when she smoothed the flat of her palm over Jane's swollen quim...once, twice, thrice.

As before, after the bath, Jane was dried and massaged with scented oil. The aroma was spicy and musky, and as the women rubbed it over her breasts, her legs, her arse, her inner thighs, its essence wafted up and mingled with the smoky incense coming from the fire. Jane tried to remain still and unaffected, but those hands slid slick and temptingly over her breasts, and came close enough to brush against her pulsing quim, and she found herself breathing heavily, twitching and straining to be touched.

At last, the torture was over—at least, in one respect—for the women released her and Jane was no longer being manipulated.

She looked over at Cold Eyes, who'd watched impassively during the entire ritual. If she had not known about his problem, she would have suspected it now, for any other man would surely have been unable to sit without participating in such a titillating scene. What she didn't know, of course, was whether his problem stemmed from the fact that he preferred men, or some other physical issue. Not that it mattered.

"Goddess. Tonight begins our formal ritual, of which you are a part. The most important part." He leered at her, and all at once Jane wasn't certain whether she was glad he spoke English or not. Perhaps she would be better off not knowing what was to happen to her.

"Will it be more satisfying than last night?" she responded boldly as the women helped her to stand. "Or do all the men in your village suffer from the same condition as you?"

His face darkened, and for a moment, she thought he might slap her. Jane shivered. *That was foolish of me.* But she was a goddess. She refused to be cowed, or to show herself as weak. These villagers might take over her body, but they could not destroy her mind and her spirit.

She would not allow it.

"It is a good thing no one else in this bloody village can understand you," Cold Eyes said, wandering over to stand next to her. The women were braiding her hair and actually putting clothing—of a sort—on her. "Or you would find yourself hanging in the sun for a week, open to anyone and anything who wished to have you."

"Tell me the truth, then: did Jonathan bring me to you? Or did he simply use my abduction as a convenient escape after we were captured?"

"Oh, he brought you here, under the guise of an abduction.

That was the agreement. He had long painted stories for us of the woman with fire hair and glittering emerald eyes and a moonlight body, spinning tales of her lusty passion and decadence. We have been without a babe in this village for nearly ten years, and the people are desperate. And so, when he learnt from the other man—Darkdale—that you had unexpectedly come to the jungle, he promised us a fertility goddess—you, the woman with the fire hair—in exchange for a map to the diamond mine he'd been seeking."

"I thought he already had a map." Jane forced herself to speak, rather than dwell on Jonathan's malevolence.

"It did not lead to the mine; it was a false one." Cold Eyes's smile, as usual, did not reach his gaze. "I made certain of it."

"And the map you gave him this time?"

"Just as false. In fact, it will lead him into the den of a mad lion, deep in the rocky mountains. I do not think you will be troubled by that man ever again. He went on his way early this morning, and I expect to hear the mad cat's roar at any time now. That particular sound carries long and far, particularly when it is satisfied."

Jane bit her lip. Poor Jonathan! Despite what he'd done to her, she didn't wish him mauled to death.

Dead, perhaps. But not dead by mauling.

"His death will also ensure no one will be looking for the red-headed Englishwoman. You and he will be presumed dead, and you will remain here with us for as long as we need you." Cold Eyes's attention skimmed over her like an icy hand. "Let us hope you bring good fortune, for the alternative will be rather unpleasant."

She swallowed, but kept her chin lifted proudly. "Beware you do not bring down the wrath of the goddess upon you."

He laughed, his eyes warming just slightly. "Tonight, I hope instead of your wrath, the village will be filled with the sounds of your cries of pleasure, goddess. For if you are pleasured, then so are all…and so will the seeds of babes be sown strongly in our women."

By now her attendants had finished their work, dressing Jane for whatever tonight's ritual was. They had adorned her hair with flowers, braiding them into her curls with vines and scented leaves, and leaving it falling in thick tresses over her chest and shoulders. Instead of pulling a tunic over her, the women draped Jane in strips of loose, soft animal skins. The effect was not so much to hide her body, but to draw attention to it—for her breasts were left mostly bare, as was the brilliant patch of red hair at the juncture of her legs. Thick cuffs, made of tanned skin, were affixed at her ankles, throat, and wrists, and when Jane noticed the large metal loops on each of them, her mouth went dry. She knew what they were for.

Just then, the sound of drums, low and thudding, came from outside.

"Come, goddess. It's time for you to meet your subjects." Cold Eyes gestured toward the door, but just as he was about to leave, one of the women said something. He froze and turned.

Jane's heart dropped. The woman was pointing to the corner of the hut where she had carefully been paring away the grass wall.

"So," said Cold Eyes, turning back to her. "You are more resourceful than I had expected. No matter. We have already prepared a place for our goddess. A cage to house our lovely bird. You will be much more comfortable there—and more securely confined."

He made an abrupt gesture and gave a command in his native tongue. Two of the women came to flank Jane, and the other three lined up behind her. The drumbeats became faster and more intense, and the ominous sound seemed to fill her ears, thudding through her body as if the drums were inside her.

She stepped forward when prodded, putting one bare foot

in front of the other as they left the hut. Jane and the women followed Cold Eyes as he walked out into the small village. The sun was low, but it was still very light outside. Nevertheless, a large fire roared in front of the same dais where Jane had originally been presented to the villagers—*only yesterday*.

The small crowd parted as the procession came through. Jane tried not to look at the hot, lascivious gazes, from both men and women, that settled on her like grabby, smothering hands. Instead, she kept her attention straight ahead. Her heart thudded, her breasts bobbed gently among the scraps of skin in which she'd been draped. Her legs rubbed against her nether lips as she walked, and she couldn't ignore their full, moist sensation.

Up onto the dais she went, the drumbeats becoming faster and harder, just as the pumping and thrusting of fucking. Jane caught sight of Devilish Grin, and looked quickly away. The very thought of that massive cock had her breath catching in her throat.

On the dais was a piece of furniture that looked like another, smaller stage. It was larger than a chair, but not as large as a table. Standing on four legs, it had a surface at hip height and was covered with furs. Standing at each corner was a bamboo pole decorated with flowering vines, their perfume heavy and sweet in the air.

Cold Eyes gestured for Jane to sit on the small platform, and she did, feeling as if she'd settled on a throne. Chanting rose around her, mingling with the drumbeats. Torches, carried by villagers, danced and streaked in the growing darkness. A scent carried by the now familiar smoking leaves filled Jane's nose and she grew warm and lightheaded.

On and on they chanted, danced, ate, and drank as she sat there, waiting for something to happen…and yet dreading whatever came next.

At last the mood changed and Cold Eyes came to stand

next to her. Jane was still unbound and unrestricted, merely sitting on her throne, and she tensed as he moved closer. But he said nothing to her, instead addressing the now silent crowd in his native tongue.

Then the villagers separated and created a sort of narrow aisle among them. A man and woman walked down the path, came up onto the dais, bowed, then sank into a kneel in front of her. Jane tensed when she realized the woman was the leader of the five who'd attended to her, but she didn't so much as reach out to touch her. Instead, her companion offered Jane a cup.

"Take it. Drink," ordered Cold Eyes when she hesitated.

Jane did as bid, lifting the cup to her lips. At first she meant to merely pretend to taste it, but Cold Eyes shoved the cup up and the liquid splashed into her mouth and over her chin. It was sweet and sticky, and tasted as though it was made from fermented berries.

"Drink it all. It is an offering," Cold Eyes told her.

She had no choice; surely they weren't intending to poison her. Perhaps it was even a drug that might dull her senses for whatever was to come. A guard took the cup after she finished drinking, and only then did the couple rise from their obeisance and face Cold Eyes. He waved an arm-length stick decorated with feathers in a sort of blessing gesture, then sprinkled them with dried leaves. Then the couple left the dais.

Another couple approached—the woman being one of her other attendants—and bowed in front of Jane. This time, she was given a plate with a small, dark square on it.

"Eat," she was told.

Another offering. Jane consumed the small square, which was a cake that tasted like dried figs and dates, along with some other element she couldn't identify. Then the couple turned to Cold Eyes for his presumed blessing. And then another couple came with a cup. And another with a special pipe. Still another with a musky-scented oil.

Jane lost count of the number of couples—there were several more than the five women who'd dressed her—and the variety of offerings, but by now the meaning had become clear: these were mates who wished and hoped for her so-called favor in their sexual endeavors.

To her surprise, none of the couples included Devilish Grin. Instead, he stood off to the side along with two other men, watching the proceeds with dark eyes.

When it appeared all the pairs had received their good blessings, Cold Eyes turned to Jane. His expression was cold and flat. "And now…for your pleasure, goddess—you must make your choice."

"Choice for what?" But her heart began to thud, for Devilish Grin and the two others he was with had come to stand before her. As before, the man in front of her fixed her with an insouciant gaze, his eyes hot and filled with promise.

Oh, God. Jane could hardly breathe. And by now, her head had begun to feel light, and her mind hazy while her body seemed startlingly awake and aware, as if the slightest breeze or the barest touch would cause waves of sensation rippling through her.

A distant roar filtered through the twilight, causing Cold Eyes to glance toward the jungle. He turned to Jane, a small smile playing about his lips. "And now we bid farewell to your man Jonathan." The lion's roar sounded again, perhaps a little closer now, and Jane shuddered, ruthlessly forcing from her mind the image of her fiancé, torn asunder and lying in a pool of blood. Her stomach lurched, helped surely by the amount of intoxicants she'd ingested, and she rose unsteadily to her feet. *Poor Jonathan.*

Cold Eyes didn't seem to have any similar regrets, and gestured to the men again. "You have the pleasure of making your choice from any of these three men. Our goddess must be pleasured. Unless…you wish to take on all three of them?"

The three candidates stood in front of the dais, bare-chested and muscular. As she looked at them, Devilish Grin whipped away his loincloth to reveal his massive erection. Jane couldn't hold back a gasp—nor control a sharp pulse from her little pip—and from the sound of it, she was not the only woman to react thus. The other two, not to be outdone, followed suit, tearing away their clothing to reveal every *inch* of their bodies as well.

Although Devilish Grin sported the largest cock, each was a fine specimen of man, and Jane actually felt weak in the knees as she considered what to do.

The only man she wanted, the only one she could have any real, deep desire for was Zaren. But her body didn't seem to understand that. As she stood there, Jane's breathing deepened and her mouth dried, while the rest of her seemed to fill and throb with anticipation.

"Very well, then," said Cold Eyes, as if to make the decision for her.

"I choose him." Jane forced the words from her lips, pointing to Devilish Grin. She'd already had his hands—and mouth—on her. And he seemed the least of the three evils. So to speak. Her belly gave a little flip as he met her eyes with hot, knowing ones.

Then, with a triumphant, jaunty smile in place, Devilish Grin vaulted onto the dais next to her. Jane turned to look at Cold Eyes. "Where shall I take him?"

"There," he said. And pointed to the throne Jane had just vacated.

She gaped at him, the blood rushing from her face. "No. Not here. Not—"

"They must to see it for themselves, goddess. All of them must see. You will show them your pleasure or suffer the consequences."

"What consequences could be worse than that?" she shot back. Her heart was thudding harder, and even though she still simmered in the midst of a pleasurable haze, her words were strong.

"Do you truly want to find out?"

Jane swallowed hard. There were many worse things that could happen, she supposed, than taking her pleasure from the man in front of her while on display. "Hanging in the sun for a week and letting anyone or anything have its way with you" was one.

Before she could respond, Devilish Grin moved behind her. He gathered up a handful of her hair, wrapping it around his fist and arm, and, using his other hand, slid it down the front of her body. Jane quivered when it came to rest between her thighs, covering her exposed mound. He stood behind her, his cock brushing the side of her hip, his warmth emanating from his dark body to her pale, white one.

"Oh." She couldn't control a gasp when he spread his fingers wide enough to cover her swollen nether lips, then began to caress and tease her. He edged a knee from behind, urging her legs to open a little more as his fingers slipped and slid through and over the folds of her quim.

Jane shivered as her body responded, tightening and filling, and when he suddenly slid a finger deep inside, she jolted and tried to twist away. But his strong hands held her firmly from behind, and she was helpless as those naughty fingers caressed and stroked and thrust inside. She couldn't hold back a moan, she panted and shivered, and still he worked—faster and faster and faster, until the pleasure exploded inside. Jane felt herself pulsing around him, against his hand, felt her slick juices covering his fingers. Her body shuddered with release and relief, and when Devilish Grin released her, she nearly collapsed.

Jane opened her eyes to find the crowd of villagers watching avidly. She was too exhausted and hazy to do more than look away and stand tall.

Thank God. It's done.

"It's done," she said haughtily, turning to Cold Eyes. "Return me to my room."

"Done? Not at all," he replied. "It's hardly begun."

Before Jane could protest, he and Devilish Grin brought her to the throne, where she had originally been seated. Instead of settling her on the fur-covered surface as if it were a chair, the two men forced her to lie on her back, feet flat on the ground. Legs spread.

Jane considered fighting them, but she knew any such action would result in her being restrained. And so she lay there, draped on another low altar, on display for the entire village…open, red, glistening, and throbbing.

She closed her eyes.

She imagined Zaren. Only Zaren, as heavy, warm hands slid down over her breasts. It was only Zaren whose hot mouth covered her exposed nipple, sucking on it and teasing it into a sharp, sensitive point. There was no one but Zaren there, and she blocked away the sounds from those who watched: the gasps and heavy breathing and even, she thought, the sounds of flesh slapping against flesh.

When the tugs of pleasure built up again, shooting from her nipple to her belly, to the tiny pearl between her legs, she imagined it was Zaren who settled between her open legs. Whose heavy, warm thighs brushed against the inside of hers, the coarse hair rough and titillating against her sensitive skin.

She felt the prod of his thick cock against her and shuddered a little—for even thoughts of Zaren couldn't completely banish the memory of its magnificent image. Her breath hitched as she imagined how it would feel, filling her, thick and long and full.

He teased her, rubbing it around and against her ready opening as two powerful hands held her hips immobile. His rod slipped and slid around, and the crowd began to cry out and chant. Jane panted, whimpering a little as he teased, then moved back, teased and moved back and around against her, giving her pleasure, but not quite enough.

Just not enough.

A sudden roar of delight from the villagers had Jane's eyes flying open, just as, a split second later, Devilish Grin slid himself inside her.

She cried out, her eyes wide and shocked. It was beyond what she'd expected. She could hardly breathe, she was so filled, so stretched, so taut and hot and wet and ready. She tried to move, to buck her hips, to get *more*, but he held her in place.

And then he shifted a little, at last, and she gasped and closed her eyes as he gave a long, slow stroke. She thought she might cry. The beginning tremor of more pleasure spiraled up inside her like a hot cyclone as he slid in, and out, and in—and then he stopped.

She cried out in frustration and need. Her nipples hurt, her skin was on fire, her quim was ready to explode.

The villagers recognized this, shouting encouragement, making animal sounds and other approving noises as Jane lay there, impaled and still. Desperate.

Devilish Grin looked down at her with hot, knowing eyes, and she opened her mouth, ran her tongue around her dry lips. "Please," she whispered, shifting her hips the little bit she was able. *Needing* him to move.

His eyes hooded, and he pulled himself back, and then *plunged* inside her. Jane screamed and he plunged again, and again, and the next thing she knew, her world was dancing in explosions and hot lights. She had no control over her body; it shuddered and wept and pulsed and burned.

And finally, *finally*, he pulled away, removing himself and his spent cock. Jane moaned and didn't have the energy to move. She still trembled with little aftershocks, and her mind was hazy.

"Very well done, goddess," said Cold Eyes.

His icy voice brought her back to the moment and Jane sat up. *It's over. This time, it must be over.*

"The people are well pleased, and for now you will be escorted to your new room—one that befits a goddess as exotic as you."

Jane was too weak to protest when her wrists were pulled in front of her belly and fastened together. Then her locked arms were brought up over her head and connected to a rope or cable above.

For the first time, she noticed the rope, dangling from a tree above them. She looked up and saw, high up in the tree, a cage-like structure. There was no way up or down that she could see, other than the rope to which she was affixed.

"Yes, goddess. You will be safe up there—safe from those who might wish to partake of your divinity, and safe from any chance you might have of escape." Cold Eyes turned to one of his men and gave a sharp command.

All at once, Jane began to rise from the dais, dangling by her wrists in the air. She spun slowly as they pulled her up, up, up toward the aerie that was to be her new accommodations.

She was halfway between the ground and the treehouse when a loud, bloodcurdling scream filled the air.

Before she could turn to see what caused it, out of the corner of her eye she saw something hurtling through the air—right toward her. She was grabbed around the waist. The next moment she was airborne, flying toward the jungle, embraced by a pair of strong, muscular arms.

Zaren.

ZAREN DREW in a deep, long breath of Jane—*Jane! at last!*—as they landed on a high branch with hardly a jolt. Below, the people who'd held her captive were shouting furiously and running about, looking up into the trees to try and spot them.

"Zaren," Jane gasped as he sliced through the rope from which she'd been hanging—the only reason he had not simply kept them slinging through the air, away from her captors. She was trembling, trying to wrap herself around him as they balanced precariously on the branch. "You came!"

Something flew through the air and embedded itself in the trunk far below them. An arrow. Her captors were not about to let her go easily.

From his treetop perch, Zaren had watched them for a long while—the way they honored her, and bowed to her, and how the one large, dark man pleasured her. His insides tightened. Perhaps she would rather stay. Perhaps she had found a new mate now that Jonathan had betrayed her.

"Jane," he said, struggling to speak, especially now that she was near him again at last, all soft, warm curves, with her heavy, fiery hair and pale, smooth skin. The strong scent of pleasure and musk and her own beautiful essence clung to her more strongly than ever, and he couldn't get enough of it. The delicious smell of her made his rod stiffen and the blood inside him sing and surge.

Jane. This was Jane. His woman.

"Oh, *Zaren*," she cried as another arrow lodged itself in a different tree. She looked up at him then indicated her wrists, still fastened together. He had them apart faster than a snake strike, and she flung her arms around his neck, pressing herself against him.

Zaren's brain went empty, and his mind went hot. He was aware of nothing but the feel and smell of *Jane.* For the moment, for now, they were safe. Despite their shouts and activity, none of those fools below could scale this tall, smooth-barked tree. Their arrows would neither shoot high enough to reach them, nor make their way through the heavy leaves and branches to find their mark. He doubted those below could even see him and Jane, surrounded by the thick greenery in the dimness of twilight.

For the moment, he had her.

"Jane…" Zaren wanted to say more, but his words dried up. She was so beautiful. So unique. So delicious. So *interesting.* He gave in, forgetting everything but the woman in his arms, pressed against him.

The next thing he knew, the trunk of the tree was behind him, solid and supporting, and he had Jane straddling his hips. Her full, pink lips covered his, her tongue thrusting sleek and hot inside his mouth. He groaned, his rod straining, ready to burst as she pushed against him, her breasts soft and lush against his chest. He was certain his heart would explode from behind its protective cage of ribs, for it was thudding so hard. His veins leapt and surged, heat filled him, dampening his skin, shortening his breath. Zaren was completely captivated by the woman in his arms: her scent, the texture of her skin, the weight of her long hair, the teasing jut of nipples, her hot, moist center—that beautiful place he dreamed of—pressed into the side of his hip.

One arm curved around her waist, holding her safe and secure, while he found a nipple with his other hand. He teased it, gently rubbing it with the pad of his finger, and felt her quiver slightly against him. He bent to kiss the side of her throat, tasting the sweetness of moist, warm skin layered with an essence of spice and oil, and buried his face in her amazing hair. Jane sighed softly, and he felt the dampness of tears on her cheek when she shuddered softly against him.

Zaren pulled back enough to look down at her in the dim light. "Jane?" He smoothed the tear away, his heart now thudding quite differently.

She smiled, her eyes crinkling at the edges, and his sudden spear of fear dissolved. "Yes," she said in a bare whisper. "Oh, yes, Zaren, please."

She reached down between them, her fingers closing around his jutting rod, and Zaren caught his breath. *Yes*, he thought. *Yes, oh yes, oh now!*

He held perfectly still, afraid that if he moved, the pleasure, the beauty of the moment, would be over in an instant. And yet, at the same time, his body strained for release, for *her*. She was his world, his very breath, the element that surrounded him now, and he wanted to join with her.

She shifted against him and her delicate finger slid around the tip of him, smoothing the small drop of moisture over the head of his insistent, raging *thing*. Blazing heat shuttled through him and his lungs became restricted. Zaren felt the tree shift beneath his feet, and he had the presence of mind to curl his toes firmly into place, to tighten his hold on Jane, even as his entire being focused on her hand, on the sensations there, where he would soon explode. Everything was there: his need, his breath, heat, arrows upon arrows of delicious sensation...

She fondled his sac, her fingers brushing through the sensitive hair there, teasing and tickling him as her hot mouth tasted his neck, his shoulder. Her tongue slid around the curve of his collarbone, into the gentle dip, then to the side of his neck. She bit him gently, as if to mark him hers, and sucked hard on his flesh as she teased that hard, throbbing part of him that was in no need of teasing.

"Zaren," she whispered, shifting against him. He felt the sudden heat and wetness of her pressing against the tip of his engorged rod, and he nearly lost his control. It took superhuman effort for him to keep his mind focused, to shift her up and into place.

When he filled her, Zaren couldn't hold back a guttural cry, a sound that was echoed by Jane. For a moment, they simply stilled, holding each other, joined, one, anticipatory.

Her hot, slick sheath surrounded him like a fist, her mouth fitted to his like a lush, sweet piece of fruit, his hands filled with curves and warmth and softness. Zaren closed his eyes, afraid to move, for he never wanted this moment to end.

It was Jane who twitched against him, who gave a little pulse around him, and his eyes flew open. Her face was right there, her eyes heavy-lidded, her mouth full and glistening, and she looked at him with the same deep *want* he felt.

He moved. She gasped and bit her lip. Zaren kissed the poor lip and moved again, and again, and again. There was nothing now but the rhythm, the heat, the slide, and the vigorous thrusting. She shuddered against him, crying out into his shoulder, and still he pumped and thrust until his very awareness shattered into wave upon wave of white-hot pleasure and release.

She trembled against him, clutching his shoulders with her hands. Skin shifted, slick and hot against the other's, their breaths mingled just as did their bodies. Zaren closed his eyes, holding her close, inhaling her familiar scent, now meshed with that of his own satisfaction and release. *Mine. My woman. My mate.*

At last, he became aware of the jungle again. Of the sounds of night birds and the predators of darkness—and of the desperate men below. Still searching for Jane.

Zaren released her, settling her onto the solid tree branch next to him. His body hummed and his knees were shamefully weak, but he must ask. He must know. It was difficult to marshal his words, his mind shattered as it was, fear tingeing the back of his mind, but he must. He drew in a deep breath.

"Jane," he said, gathering his words carefully. "You go with me?" Though he believed she had been a captive, he would not take her unless she agreed.

He would not be Jonathan.

Even in the dim light, he saw her eyes open wide. Shock. She flung her arms around his neck. "Oh, yes! Zaren, yes, I will go with you! I will go with you *always. Forever.*"

A hot burst of pleasure and joy swelled inside him, and, scooping an arm around her bottom, Zaren seized a strong vine. With Jane pressed against him—her breasts, her warm skin, the sweet-scented hair, the heat of the special, delicious place between her legs—Zaren launched them off the tree branch.

He gave his bloodcurdling yell—this one of triumph and victory—as they flew through the air, brushing against leaves and vines, disturbing birds, butterflies, and insects.

Mine. Forever.

That was his last thought before something sharp and burning hot slammed into the side of his torso.

The next thing he knew, they were falling.

Colette Gale is the pen name of a *New York Times* and *USA Today* bestselling and award-winning author who has written for three major publishers in a variety of genres.

She has also written several "seduced classics," including the popular *Unmasqued: An Erotic Novel of The Phantom of the Opera*.

Colette can be found on Facebook
(**facebook.com/colette.gale**)
or her website (**colettegale.com**)

For information about Colette's upcoming releases, please sign up for her newsletter at:
bit.ly/ColetteGaleBooks

Made in the USA
San Bernardino, CA
09 August 2015